WINNIE

Michael Edwin Q.

WINNIE

MICHAEL EDWIN Q.

Winnie by Michael Edwin Q.
Copyright © 2020 by Michael Edwin Q.
All Rights Reserved.
ISBN: 978-1-59755-600-2

Published by: ADVANTAGE BOOKS™
                 Longwood, Florida, USA
                 www.advbookstore.com

Library of Congress Catalog Number: 2020943687
1. Fiction:: African American - Woman
2. Fiction: African American – Historical
3. Social Science - Slavery

Cover Design: Alexander von Ness
Editor: nancysabitinicopyedit@gmail.com

First Printing: August 2020
20 21 22 23 24 25   10 9 8 7 6 5 4 3 2 1
Printed in the United States of America

If only it were all so simple! If only there were evil people somewhere insidiously committing evil deeds, and it were necessary only to separate them from the rest of us and destroy them. But the line dividing good and evil cuts through the heart of every human being. And who is willing to destroy a piece of his own heart?

Aleksandr Solzhenitsyn

Michael Edwin Q.

One

A Mighty Light

"Rape...Rape! Help me, someone!" she cried, her voice echoing all through Main Street.

Deputy Sheriff Henry Coleman was just dozing off when the sound of a woman shouting, 'rape!' shocked him back to life. He was resting in the sheriff's chair, his feet on the desk. When he heard the cry for help, he jumped to his feet, frantically looking for his boots.

It wasn't until he slammed the office door and took about ten steps did he realize he'd put his boots on the wrong feet. It was too late to do anything about it, now. He could only hope no one noticed.

"Help...help!" the cry continued.

Deputy Coleman ran in the direction of the shouting. Main Street was deserted; save for a few storekeepers who'd stepped out to see what the ruckus was all about. At the end of the street, a large, gruff man wrestled with a young girl. As Henry ran closer, he got a better look at them and a better idea what was going on.

By the way he dressed; the large man was clearly a farmer or plantation worker. He was trying to subdue the young woman and place her in the back of his wagon.

The young woman couldn't have been more than sixteen years old. Barefoot and dressed in a simple light brown dress, she was petite, coming up to her assailant's chest. Her shoulder-length hair was raven black, as were her eyebrows. Her skin was smooth as silk, with a slight beige hue, the color of a newborn fawn. Henry only caught a glimpse of her face, as she struggled with the large man. In that split second, he new he was looking at perhaps the most beautiful woman he'd ever laid his eyes on.

"What in tarnation is goin' on here?" Henry shouted, catching both their attention. They stopped their struggle.

The large man pointed his chin at the deputy's badge on Henry's vest. "Help me get this hellcat in this wagon," he spouted.

The young girl looked into Henry's eyes. "Please, sir, help me. This man is trying to take advantage of me. My father is Terence Cummings. I can promise you a large reward if you help me."

Michael Edwin Q.

Henry knew the name Terence Cummings, though he never met the man. Terence Cummings was the owner of one of the largest plantations in the county. Other than that, Henry knew little else about him, if he had a daughter or not was a mystery to Henry.

The large man began laughing, still holding his arms tightly around the young woman. "Don't listen to her, she's a liar. I work for Mr. Cummings. This here is one of his slaves. She's a runaway."

Henry heard stories about white slaves, except he'd never seen one.

"A white slave girl...?" Henry asked.

The large man laughed all the harder. "White girl...? I gotta admit she's the lightest darkie I ever seen. But she's a colored girl, mark my word."

"He's lying," the girl shouted, as she began to struggle again. "Do I look colored to you?"

By now, some of the townsfolk gathered around. A little boy stood with his mother, pointing at Henry's boots. Eventually, everyone was laughing at Henry's backwards footwear. It was all too embarrassing and confusing for Henry. He took his pistol out from his holster.

"All right, I'm takin' both of ya in, till we can figure this out," Henry said, waving them on toward the Sherriff's office.

"You're makin' a big mistake," the large man said, as he walked past Henry, toward the office, still holding the girl's arm.

The girl threatened Henry, as they walked on, "When my father hears of this, you'll be out of a job."

"Nice boots, Henry!" someone in the crowd shouted.

****

Sheriff Walton Douglas had been a lawman as far back as anyone in town could remember. He was years past age when most folks would give up working. With the kids grown and moved away, his wife hounded him to quit. However, folks liked him and he enjoyed the job. He knew everyone in the county and they knew him. In all his years as Sheriff, he thought he'd seen it all. That is till he stepped into the office that day. Sheriff Douglas looked at the two and only jail cells, a prisoner in each. Henry was sitting behind Douglas' desk, putting his boots on.

"What the hell's goin' on here, Henry?"

Henry stood before the two jail cells, pointing as he described the situation. "I heard this girl hollerin', so I came a runnin'. Down the street a ways, I found these two scrappin' at each other. This big guy, here, was trying to get her into the back of his wagon. He tells me he works on the Cummings Plantation, and that this here girl is a runaway black slave. I mean, Sheriff, just look at her, does she look colored to ya? So, I locked 'em both up till I could figure this all out."

Sheriff Douglas walked to the front of the far cell, looking into the eyes of the large man.

"Tom..." Douglas said in greeting. "How have ya been?"

"Good to see ya, too, Walton. I've been better."

Sheriff Douglas turned to look at the young woman in the other cell, still addressing the large man. "So, tell me, Tom, what's this all about? Who's this girl?"

"She's just another one of the slaves owned by Mr. Cummings. She was born there, twasn't bought or anythin'. She ran off about three days ago. Mr. Cummings had me go after her. Hell, I was up and down these hills, lookin' for her. It wasn't till my supplies were runnin' low that I figured to come into town and restock. And who do I see walkin' down the street like she owns the place, but little missy, here."

Douglas walked over to the cell.

"Kind of light skinned for a darkie?" Douglas aimed this question at Tom.

"I gotta admit it, Walton, she is a might light for a colored. But if ya look at her in the right light, ya can tell. She ain't foolin' anyone."

"What's your name, girl?" Douglas asked.

She ignored him.

"She's a feisty little wench," Tom advised. "Be careful, she bites."

Douglas moved in closer. "Listen, girl, if ya know what's good for ya, better answer me. Now, tell me what's ya name?"

"Winnie," she answered hesitantly.

"She told me she was Mr. Cummings' daughter," Henry added, in his own defense.

"Is that true?" Douglas asked. "Are you kin to Terence Cummings? Ya best tell me the truth, because I'm gonna find out sooner or later. Is Tom, here, tellin' me the truth? Are ya a slave or not?"

Winnie only nodded her answer.

"It ain't my fault," Henry argued, again trying to justify his actions. "How was I to know? I mean, she looks just like any white girl you'd see on the street, on any given day."

Sheriff Douglas looked careful at Winnie, and then turned to Henry. "Henry, you're about as useless as teats on a boar. I admit she's a might light, but anyone with half a brain can see she's colored. She ain't foolin' nobody."

Douglas took down the ring of keys off the wall, opening Tom's cell.

"Sorry about this, Tom. It's all been one big misunderstandin'."

"Do me a favor, Walton. Give me some rope to tie her up. She's a hell cat, is what she is, and she bites."

They tied Winnie's hands and feet. Tom carried her over his shoulder to his wagon. Walton and Henry accompanied him to see them off. Tom tossed Winnie into the back of the wagon, like a side of beef. To their surprise, she gave no resistance.

"Ya give Mr. Cummings my best, ya hear?" Douglas said, as the wagon rode off. He started back to the office, with his deputy at his heels. "Ya know, Henry, you're as dumb as a bag-a-hammers."

****

Terence Cummings was a short, fat, little man, as round as he was tall. His mustache was just the width of his pug nose. A halo of long chestnut brown hair encircled his head, accenting his bald dome. He was middle aged, with no wife, no children, no family, and no friends, and that was the way he preferred it.

Born into money, Cummings had the *Midas touch*. He'd doubled his inheritance many times over. He knew the value of a dollar, and the value of a lovely slave girl such as Winnie.

When Tom entered Cummings' office, he dragged Winnie behind him. He tossed her to the middle of the room. She stood before Cummings, her head bowed, not wanting to look at him.

"Where did you find her?" Cummings asked.

"Ya won't believe it, in the middle of town, of all places. I had some trouble with the law, some idiot deputy, but Sheriff Douglas straightened it all out. He said to give ya his best."

Cummings reached out, placing his hand under Winnie's chin; he lifted her face to meet his.

"My God, if you weren't so beautiful, I'd have you killed, right now. But I'll make some good money on that beauty. Still, you've fallen out of my graces. You must be punished. From now on you have no family or friends, no life at all." Cummings turned to Tom. "I want you to chain her to a post in the barn. She will remain there with all my other precious animals. No one is to see her or speak to her, except to bring her meals."

"No punishment?" Tom asked. "I mean, she did run away."

Cummings thought about it for a moment. Any chastisement, such as whipping, would be detrimental to her rare good looks, and diminish her salability. She was a high priced commodity, and he wanted her to remain so.

"I want you to beat her with a switch," Cummings finally said.

Tom shot a questioning look, until he heard the final command.

"The bottoms of her feet, I want you to beat her with a switch on the bottoms of her feet. That will teach her not to run away."

Tom smiled knowingly, pleased to hear the conclusion. He took hold of Winnie by the arm, and started out the door.

****

Within hours, a chain was imbedded into a far post in the barn. At the end of the chain was a shackle that locked around Winnie's left ankle.

Two men tied her ankles to a stick, which kept her legs spread far apart. While this was happening, Tom was out in the woods to the north, looking for just the right switch. It would need to be just the right size, long enough and flexible enough to slap hard against the flesh. Thick enough, to get the point across, only not to thick to cause irreversible damage, perhaps as thick as a man's thumb.

When he found just the right switch, using his jackknife, he cut it from the bush. He shaved all the leaves off, till it was one smooth switch. Then he returned to the barn.

They lay Winnie on her back; the two men lifted the stick, which raised her legs, giving them a clear view up her dress. They laughed and made slighted remarks. If truth be told, they would have had their way with her, only they knew Winnie was one of Mr. Cummings prized possessions. It was best to keep one's distance. All looky no touchy, if you knew what was best.

Tom positioned himself so he could hit the bottoms of both her feet with one swish. He brought the switch as far back as he could. The air whistled, as he quickly brought it forward. There was a loud smacking sound when the switch hit the flesh of the bottom of her feet. She went stiff as a board, her back arched high, demanding of herself not to moan or cry out.

The next hit was the same, and then another, till finally; she could bear it no longer, shouting in pain. Yet, she would not beg for mercy. She would not give them the satisfaction.

After two dozen strikes, Tom stopped. They let her drop to the ground, untying her from the stick. She lay there, covering her face with her arms, rather than let them see her cry.

"That ought to teach ya," Tom shouted down at her. Unable to resist the temptation, he kicked her in the stomach. She doubled up in pain. "Come on, boys," he said, walking away and out of the barn, followed by the other two men.

Alone, Winnie gathered all her strength to sit up, to inspect the soles of her feet. The cuts were many and as deep as if cut by a razor. She moved about on her knees. It would be weeks before she could stand on her own two feet, again.

Chapter Two

A Fair Price

Terrance Cummings was a good businessman. Commerce came natural to him. He knew how to sell and buy, and how to benefit from each, except, there was a problem with the selling of Winnie.

Whenever he sold a slave, all he need do was place an advertisement in the gazette. Something simple like *Young, strong, hardworking Negro, will take best offer,* or *Elderly Negress, experienced cook.*

That Sunday, after services, Terrance would be approached by no less than three offers from other plantation owners.

However, selling Winnie was different for two reasons.

For one, an advertisement in the gazette describing: *young, beautiful, light-skinned Negress, would make great mistress,* would not go over well, and met with protest. Most likely, the gazette would refuse to run a post concerning something of such a delicate nature, and considered risqué by many. Nevertheless, even if they did, the women of the community, or better put, the wives of plantation owners would object. It was a known fact that many plantation owners kept slave girls as mistresses. Still, it was all on the hush-hush. The mistress was always kept hidden from disapproving wife. As well as keeping the fact concealed from wives who did not approve of their husbands' actions. For though they didn't approve, they turned a blind eye, only they did not want it flaunted in public, nor anywhere within their world. Out of sight, out of mind.

Without an advertisement, the sale would have to be done through word-of-mouth. This brought up the second reason the sale of Winnie would be difficult. All of Terrence's fellow plantation owners knew all too well of Winnie's beauty, and many of them desired her, willing to pay top dollar for her. Only, they all knew of her demeanor, her rebelliousness, and natural defiance. Winnie was a wild filly that no one wanted to spend the time or money to tame.

****

Months passed without a single bid for Winnie. The wounds on the soles of her feet healed considerably. She was able to walk around, although, she was seldom allowed to go outside the barn.

Cummings was at the end of his rope. He was just about to send Winnie back to the fields to work alongside the other slaves. Believing he'd never get any serious money for her. Then out of the blue an answer appeared at his doorstep.

"There's a gentleman to see ya, sir," Cummings' fifty-two year old houseboy announced, standing in the doorway of Cummins' office.

Cummings looked up from his desk at the graying black man dressed in a dark suit and white gloves.

"Who is it?" he inquired.

"Samuel Runt is the name, sir," a man said, pushing the servant out of his way, entering the room. He was about to tell the man to get out of his office, when the man said the words Cummings was longing to hear. "I'm here to make a bid on the young Negress you have for sale."

Physically, Samuel Runt was the exact opposite of Cummings. He was tall, boney, a scarecrow of a man. His long dark hair was uncombed and unkempt. Cummings noticed the filth under Runt's fingernails, when the two men shook hands. Runt's hairless face was long, coming to a hatchet-point at the edge of his elongated nose. His eyes were milky and colorless. Dressed completely in black, he looked like a combination of a funeral director, embalmer, mortician, and gravedigger.

As much as the two men were physically different, inwardly they were quite similar. Both were conniving scoundrels with black hearts.

"Please, take a seat, Mr. Runt. I believe you're talking about Winnie, a lovely girl, I might add."

"Yes," replied Runt as he sat down. "I was led to believe that is her name. I'd like to see her, before we discuss price."

"Of course...of course..." Cummings countered, and then looking to his manservant. "Find Tom, tell him to fetch Winnie, bring her here, immediately." The servant was gone in a blink. "Bourbon, Mr. Runt?"

"Don't mind if I do," Runt replied with a crooked smile.

Two glasses of bourbon and a cigar each later; Tom entered the room, pushing Winnie before him.

The poor girl stood in the center of the room, motionless, staring down at the floor.

Runt rose from his chair, approaching her for inspection.

"Look at me, girl," he demanded.

Winnie slowly lifted her head and looked Runt in the eye. There was an air of defiance hovering between them, coming from Winnie.

"Prettiest young darkie in the state, wouldn't you agree, Mr. Runt?" Cummings said, more of an announcement than a question.

Runt ignored the comment, continuing to give Winnie the once-over, as one might do when purchasing a farm animal. He looked in her mouth, counting her teeth, feeling her here and there. Winnie gave no resistance.

Runt backed off from her. "She smells like horse manure," he announced.

"That's because we've kept her in the barn," Cummings responded.

"Why would you do that?" Runt asked.

It was clear Cummings struggled for an answer. "I didn't want her around other slaves. She's special."

From the look on Runt's face, he apparently wasn't buying it.

"It's no problem. A bar of soap and some water and the smell will be gone," Cummings added.

"I'd like to discuss price, now," Runt declared. "I'd like to do that alone, just the two of us."

"That will be all, Tom," Cummings ordered.

Tom took hold of Winnie, and left the room. When the door closed, the two men sat down, again.

"Would you like another glass of bourbon, Mr. Runt?"

Runt shook his head that he didn't. A strange occurrence, as Samuel Runt never turned down anything for free. This was business, money, and Runt wanted to remain sharp.

"I was thinking two thousand to be a fair price," Cummings proclaimed firmly, wearing a kindly smile.

Runt smiled back with a wider grin, his yellow teeth shining like a lighthouse glaring into a stormy fog. "Let me tell you how I came to be here, today. I got word from a friend of a friend that you had a lovely young slave girl for sale, untouched as I understand it. I also heard from this friend of a friend that she is a holy terror. You see, Mr. Cummings, I do this for a living. I buy pretty young things; I sell them to schools that teach these girls what they need to know to please a gentleman of quality. They, in turn, sell these girls after many months of training. So, you see, Mr. Cummings, many mouths need feeding from the same trough. And from what I've been told it will not be an easy task to mold this young girl. So, my price to you, Mr. Cummings is two hundred. Take it or leave it, sir."

Cummings huffed and puffed like an angry bull. "That's preposterous!" Cummings shouted, sounding insulted. He stood, pointing to the door. "I'm afraid I'll have to ask you to leave, sir."

Runt shrugged his shoulders, rose from his chair, heading for the door.

Before his hand was on the doorknob, Cummings made a counteroffer. "One thousand...let's say one thousand."

Runt stopped, smiling to himself. He'd done such negotiations hundreds of times. He knew he had Cummings right where he wanted him. He turned. "I told you it was 'take it or leave it', but I'm feeling benevolent. I will raise my bid to three hundred.

Cummings sighed. He knew he was between a rock and a hard place. Three hundred would never replace the money he'd already lost on the girl. However, three hundred was better than a poke in the eye with a sharp stick.

"In gold...?" Cummings asked.

"But, of course," Runt replied.

"Very well, three hundred," Cummings sadly agreed.

Runt held out his hand. The two shook on it.

Cummings' men took Winnie out behind the barn.

"Strip...!" Tom ordered her.

Winnie knew what was to happen next. Two of Tom's men stood by, both holding a bucket of water in each hand.

They each doused her with water. Soaked from head to toe, she stood shivering.

Tom tossed her a bar of soap. "Get to it, girl."

Once she was scrubbed down well and covered with foam, they tossed two more buckets of water, rinsing her off. Tom tossed her a towel to dry herself.

"Ya can put your dress back on, now," Tom said when she was fairly dry.

"Hold on," a voice said from behind. They all turned to see who it was. There stood Samuel Runt with Terrance Cummings standing behind him. Runt stepped forward, a stack of women's clothes in his arms.

"Here, put these on," Runt said, handing her undergarments, a new dress, one finer than anything she ever owned, and a pair of new shoes. Everything fit perfectly, as if Runt knew her measurements in advance.

As Runt and Winnie walked passed Cummings, he realized he'd been taken.

"You must have been pretty cocksure you were going to get her at the price you wanted," Cummings said, sounding upset.

Runt laughed, "Not really, I would have paid as high as one thousand. You would have gotten your price, if you weren't such an amateur."

One hour later, Winnie sat in the back of a carriage with Samuel Runt sitting next to her. There were two large men seated up front, one of them driving the carriage.

Winnie looked back for one last glimpse, inwardly saying good-bye to the only world she ever knew. Then she looked ahead to the world she'd only heard and dreamed of.

Chapter Three

One Big Mistake

When the train pulled into the station, Winnie's eyes went wide. She shook in terror, although she didn't show it, which she was good at. The train whistle blowing, the steam hissing, the wheels grinding to a stop tore into her ears.

On the train, she sat alone, across from Runt. The two large men sat together, a few seats away. Never at anytime did at least one of them have her in their sight. Every move she made brought them to attention.

The train rumbled as it gained speed. Again, Winnie refused to show any signs of fear. She was in awe, watching the world speeding by outside her window. She understood the world was large, yet only in hearsay, an idea in her mind, now it was made flesh.

The train slowed, as it pulled into Atlanta. She'd never seen so many people and tall buildings, in one place. The noise, hustle and bustle in the streets, was confusing and upsetting.

Winnie nearly twisted her neck looking in every direction, as they were shown through the lobby of the *Continental Hotel*. She was brought to her room, and locked in from the outside. It was a small room with one bed and a dresser, very neat and orderly. The first thing she did was rush to the single window. They were on the second floor, far too high up to make a jump for it. If she didn't kill herself, she would at the least break a leg.

She spent the next few hours sitting in a chair, staring out the window. Freedom so close, yet so far away.

There was a knock at the door, Winnie stood and faced it.

"Who is it?" she asked, timidly.

"I got your dinner, missy."

"The door's locked; I can't open it," she countered.

"That's all right, missy, I got the key, right here."

There was a jangling at the lock; the door opened. An old black man, entered, wheeling a cart before him. He was dressed in the strangest of uniforms, tan pants, and a waist length red jacket with gold buttons. He was a short, thin, frail old man. Winnie's first thought was that she could easily overcome him.

She charged toward the door, pushing the cart out of the way, food falling to the floor. The old man tried to block her. With one swift bash from her right arm, she slammed him out of the way. Falling to the floor, he hit his head, hard.

The next moment, a feeling of compassion and shame washed over her. She stopped and bent down, checking the old man. He looked up at her with sorrowful eyes.

"I was just bringin' ya dinner."

"Are you all right?" she asked, helping him to his feet, and then she began helping him take up the fallen food, replacing it onto the cart.

"I got strict orders to not let ya out. If your daddy finds out ya skedaddled, he'll have my job. I can't lose my job. Please, missy."

"He's not my father!" she shouted at him. Taking a deep breath, letting it out slowly, she regained her calm. "All right, I promise not to run away. But you have to promise to do something for me."

"What's that, missy?"

"You have to promise to tell someone about me, the police, the hotel manager, somebody. He's not my father, and I've been kidnapped. You understand? Will you do that for me?"

The old man nodded, as he backed out of the room.

"You promise?" she called to him.

"I promise, missy."

There was jingling at the lock.

Winnie returned to her chair by the window, staring out at the sunset.

****

Winnie spun around when she heard someone at the door. It opened slowly. A tall, sturdy-looking white man in a plan suit stood in the doorway.

"My name is Marigold, Mr. Marigold; I'm in charge of hotel security. I've recently learned from one of the staff that you claim you are not a guest of your own free will?"

"That is correct, sir, I've been kidnapped," Winnie declared as she stood up to face Marigold.

"What is your name, child?"

"My name is Winifred Cummings. "I'm a white girl, sir. My father is Terence Cummings. I've been kidnapped by a Mr. Samuel Runt with the intent of selling me into slavery. Please, sir, you must help me."

"Follow me," Marigold said, turning and walking toward the stairs. Winnie followed at his heels.

Downstairs, Marigold guided her to his office.

"Just wait in here. We'll get to the bottom of this," he said, shuffling her into the office, locking her in.

The first thing Winnie noticed, there were no windows. If there were, she would have been gone in a blink. Thinking, contemplating her predicament, seemed pointless. Why had she said that she was the daughter of Terence Cummings? It was a well-known name. What if they wired word that his daughter had been kidnapped and was being held prisoner in a hotel room in downtown Atlanta? She could only hope her mistakes would not come back to bite her.

A minute later, the office door opened. In the doorway stood Marigold, beside him was Runt, behind them were the two large men.

"Back to your room, girl," Runt said, backing away so the two men could take hold of her.

"You're making a big mistake," Winnie shouted at Marigold, as the two men escorted her out. "Why don't you believe me? Why do you believe this monster over me?" she cried, pointing her chin at Runt.

Marigold stopped them, looking into Winnie's eyes. "You made one big mistake, you ignorant girl. You introduced yourself as a 'white girl". 'My name is Winifred Cummings. I'm a white girl'. No one does that, except maybe a colored girl trying to pass."

The two men lugged her past Marigold, up the stairs and back to her room. Before locking her in, Runt gave her an ultimatum.

"Listen to me, and listen well. I'm only going to tell you this once. I'm a very patient man, but I do have my limits. I'm also a very rich man. I adore money. I can never get enough of it. I'm also very frugal; I hate losing a single penny. When I'm angered, I sometimes make the wrong decisions, ones that quite possibly might have me lose money. And I would lose money if I don't deliver you to your new owner. But I swear, if you try anything like that again, I'll kill you, and damn the money."

Chapter Four

The Root of All Evil

They sat on the train in the same positions they had done the day before. Runt ignored her. The incident at the Continental Hotel was over and done with, forgiven, although not forgotten.

After a few hours of traveling, Winnie leaned across to Runt, whispering, "I need to make wet."

It was a reasonable request. Runt turned, motioning for the two large men to approach. When they stood alongside, Winnie looked up at them.

"I need to make wet," she repeated, louder to be heard over the rumble of the train.

"Take her," Runt ordered.

They ushered her to the back of the car to a wooden door. One of the large men knocked on the door. When there was no answer, he opened it. Winnie entered the small room. The man stood in the doorway, making it impossible to close the door.

"Do you mind?" Winnie asked.

He looked about the closet-sized room, inspecting it. When he felt there was no need for concern, he backed away, allowing her to close the door.

It was a small space with little room to move about. It was difficult to stand, being tossed about from the swaying of the train. In one corner was a waist-high shelf on which were a pitcher of water, a basin, and a towel that had obviously been used multiple times. Above that was a small mirror.

To the left of that, a foot over, was a *Drop Chute Toilet*, which is a polite way of saying there was a hole in the floor. Could she escape through this hole? Looking down into it, she saw the tracks moving swiftly in a blur below. The chances of not being crushed under the train's wheels were slim to none.

On the outside wall was a secured metal bar, clearly for keeping your balance as you crouched over the Drop Chute. Above that was a window, an extremely small window.

Winnie wrapped the towel around her fist and punched out the glass. The thunderous sound of the rails passing below covered up the crash. Using the secured metal bar as footing, she lifted herself up and out the window. It was a struggle to slip through, the opening was so small. The tiny shards of glass that remained shred her dress, cutting into her flesh.

Finally, she freed herself, only to fly outward and down to the ground, thankfully, landing on some tall grass. From there she rolled down a hill into a gully. She was battered and bruised; the world was a shadowy haze. Nevertheless, once able to get up onto her feet, she began running – fast.

****

Winnie ran for nearly an hour straight. She ran through fields and forests, passing farms and plantations, keeping her distance. Standing at the top of a hill, she saw a small town off on the horizon. On the outskirts of town, was a small whitewashed church with a high steeple. Perhaps, there she could claim sanctuary and find asylum. It was her only chance.

Coming upon the church, all was quiet. Entering, she found it empty. As she walked up the center aisle, the floorboards wailed under her feet. A door at the front of the church opened, and the pastor entered.

He was a short, gray-haired, clean-shaven, middle-aged black man. His dark suit and stiff white collar identified him as the pastor.

"May I help ya?" he asked gently, smiling, walking toward her. He looked her up and down. Noticing her torn dress and streams of blood seeping out of the tears, his look turned to one of concern. "My dear, are you all right?"

"Please, sir, help me, please," she pleaded.

"First, let's get ya cleaned up. Are ya hungry?"

He led her through the door. There was a small apartment within. He gave her a damp towel to clean herself. Then he sat her down at a small table, serving her cheese, bread, and water. He sat down next to her.

"I'm Reverend Lugner. I'm the pastor, here. And your name is...?"

"Winifred, sir, but everyone calls me Winnie."

As she ate her meager meal, she opened her soul to Reverend Lugner, telling him every detail. She told of how she was a slave on the Cummings Plantation, how she was treated, and then finally sold to Samuel Runt.

"And where was this Mr. Runt taking ya?" Lugner asked.

"To New Orleans, to sell me to a school where they teach you to be a *Fancy...*"

"A Fancy...? What's a Fancy?"

Winnie stopped her chewing, feeling awkward. "It's a black girl taught to be the mistress for a rich white man."

"Black girl…? Was any of your folks white?"

"No, sir, this is just the way the Lord made me."

Lugner reached across the table, patting her hand in a fatherly manner. "Don't ya worry none, child. Ya are safe, now."

After sunset, Reverend Lugner brought her to his bedroom. It was a small room with and equally small bed.

"Ya can sleep here, tonight," he said, pointing to the bed.

"Oh, I couldn't' do that," Winnie said. "I couldn't take you out of your own bed."

He laughed. "That's no *never-mind.* I usually sleep in the armchair, anyways. I read the Good Book till my eyes become heavy. The next thing I know it's mornin'." He slowly closed the door. "Ya have a goodnight, dear. We'll figure what to do with ya, tomorrow."

"Thank you, Reverend Lugner."

"No need to mention it, it's just the Lord's work. God bless ya, child."

Alone, Winnie had all intentions of getting undressed before getting into bed. Only, she was so exhausted, she landed face down on the bed, and fell fast asleep.

****

The first light of the day poured slowly across Winnie's face, waking her gently. In the next moment, there was a knock at the door.

"Are ya decent?" Reverend Lugner spoke softly.

It was then Winnie realized she not only slept in her clothes, she spent the night on top of the covers.

"Yes," she called out.

The door slowly opened, Reverend Lugner stuck his head in. "May we come in?"

The question took her off guard and by surprise. Who were these *we*?

Just then, a hand gently pushed the reverend aside. In walked Samuel Runt. He stood at the foot of the bed, smiling.

"When we realized you were gone, we got off the train. Reverend Lugner, here, was kind enough to wire the station to let us know you were here." Runt took his wallet out from his inner coat pocket. He took out a few dollars, handing the wad to Reverend Lugner. "Thank you for your help, Reverend."

Winnie saw the two large men standing just outside the room. Knowing it was all hopeless, she rose from the bed, walking out of the room. She looked directly into the eyes of Reverend Lugner, as she passed him.

"Why would you do this? I trusted you!"

He quickly averted his eyes from her gaze. He didn't answer her question. She looked at the money in his hands, and understood.

There was a carriage waiting outside. Runt and Winnie got in the back, as the two large men sat up front, driving.

Winnie stared down at her hands in her lap. Runt looked out the window, as he spoke.

"It's fortunate for you that we are so close to New Orleans. We'll be there, by the end of the day. As I told you before, anger can take precedence over my love of money. If it wasn't that I will be rid of you in a few hours and have my pay in my hands, soon, you would be dead, right now. Look at me, when I talk to you!" he shouted.

Winnie looked up into his face.

"If the love of money is the root of all evil, then give me evil. Wouldn't you agree? I know the Reverend Lugner would."

Runt burst into a fit of laughter, a rare occurrence.

Chapter Five

Foolish Girl

New Orleans looked more like a fairytale village than a city. The ornate buildings, the crowded harbor, the streets swarming with interesting people coming and going, the noise, the hustle and bustle, intrigued Winnie, completely.

At the edge of the city, they came to a large property. A high stone wall surrounded the two-story mansion. The guards opened the gate, when they recognized Runt. They rode through a magnificent garden up to the front door. Again, there were guards on duty, on the porch.

Only Runt and Winnie entered the house. At the end of a long hallway was a door. Runt knocked. "It's Samuel," he announced.

"Come in, Samuel," a woman's voice called from within.

Three walls of the room were covered with shelves of books from floor to ceiling. A large window with a view of the garden was on one wall. In the center of the room was a desk. Behind it sat the most beautiful woman Winnie ever laid eyes on. Her long dark hair and deep-set eyes were in contrast to her white skin, the color of Chinese porcelain. She dressed like royalty. An air of worldliness and confidence enveloped her.

"Good to see you, again," Runt announced. He motioned both his hands to Winnie. "Is she not everything I said she was?"

Rising from her chair, she examined Winnie, carefully.

"A very lovely girl, I have to agree. But I can tell you it will be a long and difficult process. One look tells me she is crude and uncouth. Besides, I can smell her from here."

"Unfortunately, she spent the last few months locked in a barn," Runt replied. "As for her coarseness, I'm sure in your capable hands she will be worthy of any fine quality gentleman, fetching a high price."

"As I'm sure you are hoping that you will be paid by percentage of the sale."

This was not what Runt wanted to hear. He liked to be paid on delivery. Still, there was no need to look down this gift horse's throat.

"Well, I must be going. Time is money." He opened the door, leaving without as much as a glance at Winnie. "I'll wire you when I have a new find," he called back over his shoulder.

"Your name is Winnie, is it not?" the woman asked.

Winnie nodded.

"My name is Madame Charbonneau. You will always address me as Madame. Here, we will transform you into a *Fancy*, a well-groomed woman worthy of being the mistress of a wealthy gentleman. When we feel you are ready, you will be sold to the highest bidder. You must do everything you are told, and keep your nose out of everyone else's business, but your own. Do you understand?"

Again, Winnie nodded.

"Don't nod your head like a donkey. You'd best get used to answering. Again, do you understand?

"Yes," Winnie replied shyly.

"Yes…what?"

"Yes, Madame…"

"Good! Now, follow me."

Madame Charbonneau guided Winnie out of the room, down the hall, into a large parlor. There was a staircase to one side. At the foot of the stairs, a bell hung on the wall. Madame Charbonneau pulled the chord, ringing the bell. A minute later, a group of women came downstairs, gathering in the parlor. There were six women, in all. They were all black women, well dressed like Madame. One of the women was older, as the others were all young and beautiful.

"This is our new student. Here name is Winnie," Madame announced.

The other girls seems unmoved, uninterested, neither concerned nor neutral. It was just another day for them.

Madame pointed to the older woman. "This is Cora, the housemother. When I'm not around, her word is law. You will obey her as you would me." She looked directly at Cora. "I leave you to it." She turned, entering her office.

Cora stepped forward. "I expect y'all to be accepting to the new girl. Lucinda, your roommate just graduated. The new girl will room with you. Help her wherever she needs it. All right, everyone to your rooms. Dinner is in two hours."

Lucinda was a tall, willowy beauty, the image of a true African princess. Her movements were elegant, as she approached Winnie.

"Follow me," she whispered.

They all climbed the stairs, returning to their rooms. Lucinda escorted Winnie to their room.

"This is your bed. In that closet are your clothes. This is my bed, and those are my things. Don't ever touch them," Lucinda said matter-of-factly. She walked to the closet assigned to Winnie, taking undergarments, a dress, laying them on Winnie's bed. "This is what you'll wear to dinner. I suggest before you put them on, you take a bath. You smell."

"I'm sorry," Winnie said in a low voice.

"Don't be," Lucinda said with the upmost seriousness. "Don't ever be sorry for anything."

****

Days flowed into weeks. Every minute was used as a learning moment. Winnie, as with the other girls, received instruction on every aspect of life, always moving forward to produce the perfect Fancy. Fashion and style were important, grooming, what to wear, hairstyles, perfumes, their looks were highly essential. They were taught to read and write - a crime in many parts of the south. Conversation was important, as well as being a good listener. Meals were a lesson in etiquette.

There were also classes concerning intimacy with a man, ways to satisfy a man's sexual appetite. This was the awkward part of the day. Cora was always the teacher of such matters. The language and descriptions made for many moments of embarrassment for most of them. Though some of them took to it like a duck to water. Lucinda never seemed fazed by it or anything else, for that matter. Thankfully, these classes were nothing more than instructions and discussions. A virgin is highly prized, jacking up the price of a Fancy. For this reason, there were never any hands-on instructions.

Madame Charbonneau was rarely seen. Except for mealtimes, when she would sit at the head of the table, constantly and carefully observing. During the meal, she would question each girl on a multitude of subjects, clearly evaluating their progress.

As for socializing, it was seldom and short. After so much time together, Winnie still found it difficult to remember some of the girl's names. Only late at night, when everyone was in their rooms, and the lights were out, did Winnie lie in bed, speaking in the dark to Lucinda. Every night, for weeks, Winnie poured her heart out to Lucinda; telling her everything about her past, every nook and cranny of her mind and heart. Why she did this, Winnie only assumed it made her feel less lonely in such a lonely situation.

Strangely, Lucinda never spoke, only lying in bed, on the other side of the dark room, listening. That is till one night Winnie grew weary of their one-sided conversations, demanding Lucinda open up to her, as she had done.

Winnie could see the outline of Lucinda as she sat up on the edge of her bed, on the far end of the room. The dull light from the window haloed around Lucinda.

"You foolish girl, you actually believe I'm your friend? Well, I'm not your friend, and I never want to be. Every night, you take me into your confidence, as if any of it matters to me. All I can do is shake my head at such a foolish girl."

"What do you mean?" Winnie questioned, sounding defensive.

"You're not realistic; you live in a fantasy world. You trust everyone and everything. Yours is a dream world."

"What do you mean?" Winnie repeated.

"You trusted the law, when you were caught downtown. No one spoke up for you. You trusted your family and friends. Where were they when you were locked in the barn? You trusted the hotel security, and he turned you over to your captives. And foolishly, you trust the Reverend Lugner to protect you. He betrayed you for a handful of silver, your own personal Judas. But worst of all, you trust God!"

"You shouldn't say things like that!" Winnie protested.

Lucinda laughed, "You really are living in a dream world. Where was God when you were born a slave, when you were taken from your family, when you were brought here to benefit someone else? Your entire life has been for the benefit of someone else. There is no God. Even if there is a God, he's either powerless or he doesn't care. If you pray to this God or nothing at all, your chances of getting what you want are the same. Wake up! The only person you need to believe in is yourself."

"But without God there's nothing, no morals," Winnie argued.

"And what are morals?" Lucinda shot back. "Nothing more than laws laid down by men to keep others in line. They're as much a fantasy as your God.

"If you want something, you take it. If someone gets in your way, kill them. Lie, cheat, steal, whatever it takes. No one else is going to do it for you. Because, when all is said and done, you're the one who's going to lie in your grave, not them.

"If you need a god so much, know that you are god. You are your own god. The self, that is who you should worship, who you should sacrifice to, who you should put above all others.

"You're a beautiful young girl in the perfect place for any girl to get whatever she wants. These opportunities are not available to black girls, such as us. Take advantage of it. You can get anything you want. The world around your finger, for giving a man a few seconds of pleasure, it's your choice. Make the best of it. Or are you going to continue whining and praying, hoping to be saved…by whom? By some gallant knight in armor, or a god who doesn't exist. As for me, I'm going to take and enjoy everything I can get my hands on. Now, say your prayers and go to sleep, and live the pitiful life you've chosen, you foolish girl."

"I'm not a fool," Winnie objected.

"We'll see...we'll see," Lucinda laughed, lying back down, turning onto her side, and closing her eyes.

Six

Seize the Day

Winnie always admired Lucinda, looking up to her, emulating her in everyway, whenever possible. Which was why, Lucinda's late night speech impressed her deeply. She took Lucinda's philosophy to heart. It was not a renouncing of God, per say. For there is no need to renounce what you don't believe exists. Winnie vowed to live for herself alone. All her old concepts of good and evil were swept away. From then on, anything that furthered her ambitions was good. Everything else was bad, something to be ignored, or crushed whenever possible.

After only a few weeks of adopting this new libertine philosophy, Winnie noticed a dramatic change in her life for the better. When once she had prayed to God for her needs, as Lucinda explained, this did not always bear fruit. Whereas, now, suddenly and mysteriously with nearly no effort, all of her wishes were made real.

Whenever she saw something she wanted, she stole it. When confronted with a house infraction, she lied, often placing the blame on one of the other girls. This made her very unpopular. Still, what did she care? She no longer needed or cared about anyone save for herself. In time, she even grew to mistrust Lucinda, and rightfully so.

Early one morning, Madame Charbonneau gathered Cora and the others in the parlor.

"I have an important announcement to make," Madame said. "One of our students is graduating. Lucinda has been purchased by a very wealthy gentleman, living right here in New Orleans."

All eyes turned to Lucinda, followed by a small polite applause.

"When are you leaving?" Winnie asked softly.

"Within the hour," Lucinda smiled.

It felt like the entire world collapsed on Winnie. Despite her new independence, Winnie feared losing Lucinda. It would truly be a lonely existence without her one friend, trusted or not.

Winnie watched from the upstairs window, as a most elegant carriage pulled up to the mansion. Two footmen loaded Lucinda's trunk atop. They held the carriage door for her. Winnie waved, hoping Lucinda would gaze up for one last good-bye. She entered the carriage, never looking back. Winnie watched them drive through the front gate and then out of view.

A month later, Lucinda returned for a visit. She came for dinner, sitting next to Cora at the head of the table. The visit was arranged by Madame Charbonneau. It was the perfect motivation for the others. Lucinda was a sight to behold. As finely dressed as they all were, it was nothing compared to what Lucinda wore. There were rings on her fingers, and pearls around her neck. Her hair was professionally styled. She looked like a princess, even outshining Madame.

After supper, Winnie got a chance to speak with Lucinda before she left.

"You...you look wonderful!" Winnie said in awe.

"You understand, now?" Lucinda asked. "I rose higher than any black woman could ever imagine possible. I have the best of everything. I give the man a few minutes of pleasure every few days, and he gives me my heart's desires. He treats me like a queen, even better than he does his wife. Follow your dream, take charge of your life, and put yourself before anyone else. You're the one who's going to die, when it's time for you to die. You are your own god. Carpe Diems...seize the day!"

****

It was not a long time later, Winnie and the others nearly forgot about Lucinda. Her name was seldom mentioned. That is until one day in class, before Cora entered the room, all the girls were whispering among themselves.

"What is it?" Winnie asked.

"You haven't heard?" one of them said. "Lucinda is dead!"

Winnie was speechless.

The girl continued, "She turned up pregnant. She tried to get rid of it. She bled to death."

"Quite! That's enough jabbering," Cora said, entering the room.

Winnie's mind was in a whirlwind of confusion. Was Lucinda's death the wrath of God, cutting the girl down for her wicked ways? Or was it all meant to be, and Lucinda should count herself lucky that she found some happiness in the world, even if it was for just a brief moment?

Seven

Jolene

Winnie enjoyed having the bedroom to herself, although she knew it would not last. She understood at some point a new girl would come, taking up the bed that was once Lucinda's. However, she never expected someone like Jolene.

Physically, Jolene was a perfect candidate to be a Fancy, young and beautiful. Inwardly, she was all wrong, the exact opposite of what Winnie had become. She went around quoting the Bible from memory, praying throughout the day, innocent, forgiving and honest to a fault. Surely, the girl wouldn't last very long, if not for the help of Winnie.

Against her better judgment and life philosophy, Winnie was drawn to Jolene, wanting to care for her as an older sister would for her younger sibling. Still, there were times; Jolene was determined to do things her own way, only to meet with the consequences of her actions.

So, Winnie set on the mission to enlighten her misguided little sister.

Late one night, as the two lie in the dark on their beds, Winnie whispered across the room to Jolene. It was the same speech she received from Lucinda, nearly word for word, for it was written in her heart.

When she finished, she felt good within, believing she had made another convert to the true path in life. She'd saved her little sister from the shortcomings and pitfalls of the wicked world. Only, to her surprise and disappointment, Jolene was not moved, purposing a counter to each of Winnie's declarations.

Jolene spoke softly, gently with a slight tremor, as if she were on the verge of tears. Her words floated across the room to Winnie.

"Oh Winnie, you are so wrong. And the sad thing is that you know it. In your heart of hearts, you know what's right and true. You're just afraid. You should never be afraid. If everyone put themselves first before everyone else, we would all lose. There is right and wrong, and there is a loving God!"

"You don't know that for sure," Winnie snapped back.

"It doesn't matter, really," Jolene said to Winnie's surprise. "If you are right, and there are no morals, no right or wrong, no god, nothing after this life, when I die it will mean nothing to me. If there is nothing but this world, then I will lie in my grave, not wishing I'd lived my life differently, believing I've stolen from myself. I won't complain or feel slighted, because there is nothing. It won't matter, because nothing matters.

"But if I am right, then everything matters. And when you die, you are looking at an eternity of regret. Winnie, turn away from this foolishness! It is never too late. God will forgive. As long as there is life, there is hope. Please, Winnie, reconsider. You are my treasured friend. Heaven won't be the same without you."

Now, Jolene was crying, heavily. Winnie's heart went out to her. She got out of her bed, walking across the room, sitting on the edge of Jolene's bed. Jolene sprang up into Winnie's arms, sobbing.

"There...there," Winnie whispered, holding Jolene close. "I'm sorry I upset you so. I promise I will at least think about it."

This seemed to relieve Jolene. Winnie tiptoed back to her bed. Staring up at the ceiling, she wished she hadn't promised to consider what Jolene told her. Now, the voices of Jolene and Lucinda were echoing in her mind.

****

It was all Winnie hoped and worked for. She was to graduate, to be sold as a mistress to a wealthy gentleman in New Orleans. She knew if she played her cards right all her dreams would come true.

Still, the battle of good and evil waged war within Winnie, though never did she dare to choose a side. Yet, it all came to a head, the last night at the school for Winnie, when Jolene asked her for a favor only a true friend, a sister, would consider.

Jolene confessed to Winnie she tried to escape. She told her how late one night, when everyone was asleep; she took one of the dining room chairs to the outside wall, trying to scale it. Sadly, she was too short, even leaping from the chair, to grasp the top of the wall.

"I can do it with your help," Jolene pleaded.

"Do you understand what you're asking?" Winnie told her. "If we're caught, it is the end of both of us. Unlike you, I finished with my studies, I stand to graduate. I'm already sold, and perhaps I can live a life worth living. One day, I will be a rich woman. So, if we're caught, that all gets taken from me."

"Then come with me," Jolene added.

"And what, throw the chance of a better life away so you and I can spend years on the run? When they catch us, and they will catch us, the best we could hope for is to be sold to a plantation, and spend the rest of our lives as slaves. They could kill us, you know?"

"You're already a slave," Jolene declared. "You're a slave to your sin. Come with me Winnie; trust in the Lord. He will save us and your soul."

"And where does this soul reside?" Winnie demanded, pointing to herself. "Where in this body is it? Can you show it to me?"

"It's more real than anything on this earth," Jolene proclaimed.

Winnie thought for a moment.

"All right, I'll help you on the condition you stop all this God-talk."

"I'll never stop praying for you, Winnie."

"Fine, just keep it to yourself."

****

Late that night, Winnie and Jolene crept from their room and down the stairs, keeping close to the wall to prevent the wood floor from creaking. They took one of the dining room chairs, stealing their way to the outdoors. Thankfully, the guards were at the front gate, none of them on the grounds. The wall was too high to scale, for one person, alone, that is.

Placing the chair against the wall, Winnie got up on the seat, her back braced against the wall. Jolene joined her.

"You ready? Winnie whispered.

"Wait, not yet," Jolene said.

"Having second thoughts?" Winnie asked.

"No," Jolene replied. "There's something I want to say."

"Not now, Jolene. We don't have the time for long good-byes. Just get over the wall and run."

"I want you to know how much this means to me. I want to tell you how much you mean to me."

"That's fine, now get over this wall."

"You are the sister I never had, and I love you."

Despite the danger, in spite of all that was at risk, regardless of loss, this stopped Winnie in her tracks. Jolene's words went straight to her heart like an arrow. It moved her to tears that anyone loved her. Never hearing the words before by anyone, including her mother, she'd long since believed it an impossibility.

"I love you, too," Winnie echoed.

In tears, the two women hugged good-bye.

"Shall we ever meet again?" Jolene asked.

"It's a big world, and I've known stranger things to happen," Winnie replied. "Besides, how many Fancy Girls can there be? Of course, we'll meet again. I'll be there when you least expect me. I'll turn up like a bad penny."

Winnie cupped her hands at her knees. Jolene placed her foot in the hand-cradle, holding tightly onto Winnie's shoulder, and then the wall.

"You ready?" Winnie asked. "On the count of three...one...two...three...push!"

Winnie thrust upward as Jolene leaped. Her fingers barely touched the top ledge of the wall. Unable to get a hold, Jolene fell backwards onto the ground.

"Are you all right?"

"I'm fine," Jolene responded.

"Quick, let's try again," Winnie said, reaching down to Jolene.

When they were back in position, Winnie gave the count.

"Again...one...two...three..."

With one tremendous effort by both of them, Jolene took hold of the top of the wall. Winnie continued to push. Inch by inch, Jolene shimmied up the side of the wall. Finally, she was able to bring one leg up. From there, she made her way onto the top of the wall.

Sitting on the edge, she stopped for a moment, looking down at Winnie.

"Are you sure you won't come with me?" Jolene asked one last time, reaching her hand down.

This was the moment of truth, time to make a decision, a life changing decision. It would have been easy to reach up, Jolene helping her over the wall. However, it was just as easy, if not easier, to go back to bed. Winnie was confused; both choices had their pros and cons.

"No, you go on without me," Winnie said, smiling.

"Are you sure?"

"Yes, I'm sure."

"I'll pray for you," Jolene said, her words falling down on Winnie like a gentle rain. Jolene turned and jumped, landing on the ground.

"Are you all right?" Winnie called out.

"I'm fine," Jolene called back.

"Jolene...my sister...good luck...."

"Winnie...my sister...God bless you."

Winnie returned to the mansion; put the chair back to its place in the dining room. Slow, she made her way upstairs to her room.

Lying in her bed, she couldn't sleep. Her mind was racing. She would have to be on her wits in the morning. There would be many questions to answer, many lies to tell. Only, that was not the only thought that kept her awake. The voices of Lucinda and Jolene were battling in her mind. Winnie knew the debate would continue until she made a decision, choosing one over the other.

Chapter Eight

First Day is Always the Hardest

"Where is Jolene?" Cora demanded, standing in the bedroom doorway.

Her head under her pillow, Winnie continued to fake sleep.

"What...what is it?" Winnie murmured, sitting up, rubbing her eyes.

"Where is Jolene?"

Winnie looked across the bedroom, as if she expected to see Jolene in her bed, and then acting surprised.

"I have no idea."

"Get dressed," Cora ordered.

Five minutes later, the bedroom door swung open, Winnie was only halfway dressed.

"I'm almost ready," Winnie declared.

"Where is Jolene?" Cora insisted.

"I told you, I don't know."

"Get dressed; meet me in Madame's office." Cora slammed the door shut.

Fifteen minutes later, Winnie stood before Madame and Cora.

"We've searched everywhere for Jolene," Madame said. "Obviously, she's escaped. What do you know about this?"

"Nothing, Madame...if she escaped, she did it in the middle of the night, while I was asleep. I know nothing about it. I swear."

"You better not be lying."

"Why would I lie, risking all that I stand to gain? For some snotty-nosed Bible-thumping little brat...it's not likely!"

Winnie knew Madame had no reason not to believe her. Besides, she was planning to make a small fortune on Winnie, that very day.

"Very well," Madame continued. "Your new owner is sending a carriage for you within the hour. Return to your room, pack your things, and prepare yourself."

"Yes, Madame," Winnie answered, turning to leave the office.

"Oh, and Winnie," Madame stopped her. "Your new owner paid a good amount for you. Remember your lessons, and make him happy. If not, I will have to return his money, and he will return you to me. I don't enjoy losing money. Bear in mind, we don't offer second chances here."

****

For whatever reason, Winnie was never told who her new owner was, it was all kept hush-hush. Winnie could only hope that it was someone somewhat presentable. After all, she was to be his mistress. A foul smelling, fat, old man would be a nightmare. Her only hope would be his age would prevent him from being too demanding. On the bright side, it could just as well be a young, handsome man, who'd treat her well. Either way, she had resided to make the best of it.

To her surprise, it was not a fine carriage that came to fetch her. It was a public carriage, a cab, which were for hire in the better parts of the city.

There were no good-byes, no one to see her off.

It was a short ride to the outskirts of the city, and then stopping in front of a magnificent two-story mansion with a fully covered porch encircling it. The finest of materials were draped in every window. The mansion sat twenty feet from the street; a waist-high picket fence separated the building from the world. A serpentine walkway to the front steps meandered through a fragrant rose garden.

Winnie was confused. It was a well-known fact, a Fancy, a mistress, would be given an apartment, not far from her benefactor. It was unheard of a Fancy living with him in his own home, especially if he had a wife and family.

"Are you sure this is the correct address?" Winnie asked the cabbie.

"Of course, it's the correct address. I ought to know my own job!" he snapped at her. There was arrogance in his voice, sounding judgmental. He seemed put-off, as he carried her bags to the front door. Obviously, he knew something she didn't, which frightened Winnie.

He pounded on the door. A moment later, a short, stout, elderly black woman, dressed in a maid uniform stood in the doorway. She looked at the cabby and then at Winnie, making an assessment.

"It's all right; it's the new girl," she shouted to whomever was behind her. "Come on in, girl," she told Winnie.

The cabbie placed the suitcases on the floor past the threshold, as Winnie stepped inside. The cabbie stood there, staring at the maid.

"Well?" she said. "Ain't ya been paid, yet?"

"Yes, I have," he remarked, clearly hoping for a tip.

"Well, don't expect any extras," she said, slamming the door in his face.

Winnie eyed the surroundings, a chill of disappointment and fear seized her. Looking into the parlors to her right and left, she understood where she was. Both rooms were filled with well-dressed white gentlemen, and scantily clad women. They were all young women of great beauty. This only meant one thing. Winnie was sold to a brothel.

"Pick up your things, and follow me to your room," said the old woman.

Carrying her suitcases, Winnie followed her up the stair, down the hall, to a door. The woman opened the door and stepped inside.

"This will be your room. Get yourself settled. I'll be back for you in a half hour," the maid said, in a matter-of-fact tone. Then she left.

It was a small room with just enough room for a single bed and a dresser with a water pitcher and basin on top. There was a tilted full-length mirror, as well, in the corner, next to the only window.

Winnie sat on the edge of the bed, her face in her hands, crying.

****

Madame Putain was a shrewd businesswoman, owner and manager of the *Club de Messieurs* in New Orleans for nearly ten years. She knew all the ins and outs of the business, having started as a woman of the evening, herself, when she was much younger. Now, middle-aged, she ran one of the most profitable bordellos in the state.

She was a short woman, standing at five-foot. A full-figured woman, busty, her hair piled high giving the impression she was taller. She was always well dressed, multiple bracelets clinking and clanging on both wrists, and diamond earrings. She wore three long strands of pearls around her neck that dangled across her large breasts swaying to and fro with her every move. She was a no-nonsense woman, letting you know that she was the moment you met her.

Winnie stood in the center of Madame Putain's office, facing the Madame seated behind her desk. It was clear Winnie was not happy to be there, her face full of disappointment and a look of defiance. Realizing this, Madame Putain decided to nip it in the bud by putting her foot down and laying down the law, from the very start.

"I run a tight ship, here, missy. This can be a good life for you, or it can be hell. You need to decide right now. It's up to you. There are two ways of doing things, here, the right way or the wrong way, my way or your own. I can tell you right now, my way is far preferable.

"You don't have to be friendly to the other girls, but I don't tolerate *Cat-Fights*. If you've got a disagreement with anyone, you come to me first.

"Your room is your room. You can decorate it anyway you want. You will see all gentlemen callers in your room. When you're not busy, you will be down in the parlor, making the guest comfortable and drumming up business."

""I've never done this," Winnie interrupted.

"No, but you've been trained, so I've been told, and paid plenty for your expertise. You make love with one man once a day or a bunch of men everyday, in the scheme of things, there ain't much difference."

"But, I'm a virgin," Winnie insisted.

"I should damn well hope so!" Madame Putain shouted, pounding her fist on her desk. Her eyes stern, as her bulldog cheeks quivered under both sides of her jaw. "I paid a pretty penny for a virgin and I best have got one. In fact, I'm going to have some of my ladies check you, later. And you better be a virgin, or I'm sending you packing. And that tramp Charbonneau better pay me back what I dished out and more.

"Now, today is Wednesday. Take the next few days to settle in. Saturday night, I'm throwing a big party. We gonna auction you off to the highest bidder. I spent big bucks for you. A light colored virgin should bring in a pretty penny. I should make most of my investment back, if not all of it.

"That's all...you're dismissed," Madame Putain said bluntly, picking up her pen, returning to the books and papers sprawled across her desk.

Winnie quietly returned to her room. She began to unpack. A few minutes later, there was a knock at her door. Before she could ask who it was, the door opened. The maid that met her at the door earlier and another maid, similar looking, entered the room.

"It's time to put up or shut up," said the first woman. "We're here to make sure ya are what ya say ya is. Now, just lie down on the bed, and try to relax."

Winnie did as she was told. She turned her head, staring at the wall, biting her lower lip.

They were quiet and gentle; however, it was still too embarrassing for words.

"Well, ya is what ya say ya is. I'll let Madame Putain know. Get ya'self cleaned up and come on downstairs."

They softly left the room, closing the door behind them. Once again, Winnie began to cry, this time loudly.

There was a knock at the door.

"Go away," Winnie shouted at the door.

"You're the new girl?" a woman's smoky voice seeped through the door. "The first day is always the hardest."

The door slowly opened. A tall, lean white woman stood in the doorway. She was dressed in all white, her strawberry blonde curls just touching her shoulders.

"Don't cry, honey. It's always darkest before the dawn. It's got to get better."

Winnie sat up, rubbing her eyes.

"I felt the same as you do when I first came, havin' no friends and all. But see you got a friend, now. I'm in the room right next to y'all. My name's Candy. What's yours?"

"My name's Winnie."

"Winnie, that's sure a cute name. Why don't you come down to the kitchen with me and get somethin' to eat."

"I'm sorry. I just don't feel hungry, right now," Winnie said, adjusting her skirt.

"I understand," said Candy. "Well, I hope you feel better. Remember if you need a friend, because you got one now, or you just wanna talk, I'm right next door. You can just bang on the wall and I'll come runnin. Life's better with a friend."

"Thanks," Winnie said softly.

Candy waved, as she backed out of the room, closing the door. From the light in the hallway, Winnie got a better look at Candy.

She was perhaps the tallest woman Winnie ever saw, slender and smooth as Crape Myrtle in September. Her blue eyes were milky. Her face was painted, her cheeks and lips unnaturally red. One of her most uncommon features was her Adam's apple. Winnie had met many women with large Adam's apples, as well as men, although, Candy's throat housed a museum sized specimen.

Winnie realized she'd stopped crying. Candy was right. Life's better with a friend, and now she had one.

Nine

The Auction

Saturday took forever to come, and when it did, it came too soon. All business stopped at noon to prepare for the evening's festivities. All furniture in the main parlor was taken out to make more room. More lamps were brought in for more light. A riser was placed against the far wall to be used as a stage.

Only the high-rollers of the city were invited, none of the riffraff, only big spenders.

Whiskey Bars were set up offering free drinks. Nothing loosens a man's tongue and purse like free drink. The kitchen was off for the night, no food would be available. Nothing sobers a man like food and time.

The entire afternoon, a league of women prepped Winnie for her big night. They spent hours on her hair, dressing her in a lovely gown, only used on special occasions.

"Good work, ladies," Madame Putain announced as she entered the room, eyeing Winnie. "Come with me; I need to speak with you," she said, pointing to Winnie.

Winnie followed Madame Putain down the hall to a room at the front of the house. She opened the door, entered, Winnie as well.

It was a large bedroom, four times the size of Winnie's. There was an overly large bed against one wall, a red silk canopy above it. The bed faced three large windows that looked down on the rose garden in the front of the house. To one side of the room was a small fully stocked bar. To the other side of the room was a collection of a dozen mirrors on stands, of different shapes and sizes. No great imagination was needed to presume what they could be used for.

"This will be your bedroom for tonight only, of course. And let me make everything perfectly clear. Tonight, during the auction, you will stand next to me the entire time. I want you smiling like it's your wedding day. The highest bidder will get you for the night, in this room. I don't care if the highest bidder is a monster with three eyes and a tail, you will act pleased and excited.

"Another thing, I want him to leave this room in the morning believing his money was well spent. Remember, it may be my money riding on this party, but it's your life on the line. Do you understand?"

Winnie nodded.

"Good! Now, get back to your room and wait till you're called."

****

Early evening, the guests started to arrive. From the looks of their carriages and servants, it was obvious these were men of means, politicians, bankers, businessmen, plantation owners, and the like.

Madame Putain hired a small group of musicians who played marching tunes. Trumpets and Trombones blared along with pounding drums. There must have been at least one hundred and fifty men, shouting, laughing, and drinking. The atmosphere was carnival like. The whiskey flowed like a river, which was what Madame Putain wanted. This went on into the early part of the night. When Madame Putain felt the anticipation was high enough, and the crowd was drunk enough, she stood on the platform, shouting to get their attention.

"Settle down, gentlemen, settle down!" she hollered.

"I bid a thousand dollars, sight unseen," a drunk shouted from the back.

"A thousand dollars…? You couldn't even get me for a thousand dollars," Madame Putain countered. They all laughed, slowly going silent.

Just then, one of Madame Putain's security men escorted Winnie to the platform. She was met with cheers and jeers, and whistles. She stood next to Madame Putain, her head bowed in shame.

"Head up…now, smile…and remember…" Madame Putain whispered into Winnie's ear.

Winnie did her best to comply; she held her head up, although the smile on her face was visibly forced. Not that it mattered to the crowd; few were looking at her face.

"Settle down, gentlemen; let's start the biding at one thousand."

A hunched over, frail old gentleman, standing upfront, raised his hand. "I bid one thousand."

Madame Putain smiled down at the old man. "Why, Matthew, what's an old codger like you going to do with a beautiful young girl like this?"

"I'm gonna stare at her all night long, and from this day on and for the rest of my life, I'm gonna lie to everyone I meet about what happened."

They roared with laughter. Madame Putain held up her hands, trying to regain order.

"Think of it, gentlemen. An entire night of bliss with this beautiful, young, virgin, negress, and I guarantee she's a virgin."

"She don't look none too colored to me," someone hollered from the back.

"Will the gentlemen care to examine her?" Madame Putain shouted.

He made his way to the front and onto the stage. He took his time groping Winnie, to whistles and jeers.

"Well, sir, what say you?" Madame Putain asked.

"She's either the lightest colored I ever seen, or she's the darkest white girl I ever seen."

Again, the crowd burst into laughter.

"Is she colored or is she not?" Madame Putain pressed the question.

"She's colored, all right," he admitted. "You gotta get up close, but she's colored, for sure."

There was a long sigh from the gathering, accompanied by oohs and aahs.

"Back to the biding," Madame Putain announced.

"Why can't we see what we're biding on?" someone shouted. "Make her lift up her dress!"

"Go on, girl, lift up your dress," Madame Putain ordered.

Winnie took hold of her skirt, lifting it slightly.

"Higher...higher...!" the crowd shouted.

She lifted the skirt to her knees, beyond that all one could see were her bloomers. Yet, it was evident to all how shapely she was. This satisfied the mob, which is what they had become. The forced smile left Winnie's face.

Over the next half hour, the biding increased in increments of one hundred or more, till the final bid was ten thousand.

"Do I have any other bids?" Madame Putain shouted. "I have ten thousand going once...twice...sold!"

The crowd roared. The band began to strike up a stirring march. The liquor was no longer free. Many of the men went about looking for some of the other house girls to work off their frustrations.

As for Winnie, the world became a blur. She remembered being taken upstairs to the large bedroom. She waited for the top bidder, the winner, to claim his prize. As soon as the bedroom door opened, Winnie's consciousness faded away like the flame of a candle being blown out.

To her, he was a man with no face. She was aware of the cold night air on her naked flesh, of being thrown down onto the bed, his heavy weight pressing her down, and his whiskey breath puffing into her face like a steam engine.

She turned her head, looking out the window, concentrating on the full moon in the sky. There was nothing in her world except her and that full moon. She tried to memorize every crevice. Was there really a man in the moon? Was he looking back at her? Did he see what was happening? Did he care?

There was a time when she would have cried through the entire ordeal. Now, she refused, going deep within herself, ignoring it as much as possible.

There was also a time when she would have prayed to God to send down mercy. Except, that was the path she'd vowed to ignore. The battle between Jolene and Lucinda that was waging in her mind had come to an end. Winnie chose the path Lucinda offered. If there was a God, he was either powerless or he didn't care. If there was a God, she hated him. She was her own god. She would see herself through all this, and come out the other end victorious.

****

In the morning, Winnie found she was alone. The man was gone. The entire house was quiet. She dressed, and made her way to her room. As she moved, she was aware of the discomfort caused by last night.

In her room, Winnie sat on the edge of her bed, staring at the floor. The bedroom door opened. It was Candy, standing in the doorway, wearing a thin nightgown.

"Are you all right?" Candy asked softly.

"I'm fine," Winnie replied, still staring a hole in the floor.

Candy entered the room, sat down next to Winnie, and placed her arm gently around her.

"You know, if you need to cry…?"

"I'm not going to cry," Winnie insisted.

"Whatever," Candy said. "I'm here for you, if you need me."

Candy stood up, heading for the door.

"My word, you are beautiful," Candy said in admiration. "I wish I had your looks, I could rule the world."

"You can have the world, as far as I'm concerned," Winnie responded.

"Well, I'll be in my room, if you need me," Candy said.

"Oh my…oh my…" Winnie said, pointing at Candy.

Candy looked herself over. "What's the matter, I got spinach caught in my teeth?"

"You don't….you don't have any breasts," Winnie declared, still pointing at Candy.

"Only the store-bought kind, honey," Candy laughed. "And I never wear them to sleep."

45

"I don't understand," Winnie said, bewildered.

"You dear child, you are as innocent as a lamb, ain't you?"

Still laughing, Candy opened her gown, exposing a thin flat chest.

"My goodness, you're a man!" Winnie stated in astonishment.

"I don't like to think of it that way," Candy said. "But I've been described in that manner a few times."

"But...how do you...?"

"Where there's a will there's a way," Candy giggled. "I always tell the gentleman as soon as they approach me. You'd be surprised how many men like that sort of thing. They'll pay twice as much as they would for a R.G."

"R.G...?"

"A real girl..." Candy slowly closed the door. "Try to get some sleep. It's Sunday. Madame doesn't expect us to start working until four."

Ten

It All Happened At Once

Weeks turned into months. Each day dragged on slowly, a repeat of the day before with little hope of change in the future. Winnie saw no prospect. Something needed to be done, only what?

She was not mistreated. She was fed well, and there was much leisure time. Besides, her friendship with Candy, she made no friends. The working girls of the *Club de Messieurs* were civil to one another, however camaraderie and familiarity was in short supply.

The one saving grace was Winnie learned to distance herself from what was happening around her and to her. Starting with the night of the auction, Winnie was able to shut the door of her mind. After months as a working girl, she could not recall one incident.

At the end of the day, as she lie on her bed, alone in her room, she'd look back on her day, only to evoke a sea of nameless and faceless men.

It was late in the night. What day of the week, Winnie could not recall; all her days looked the same to her. The crowds had left, the music stopped, the house was growing silent, as everyone bedded down, calling it a night.

Sprawled out on her bed, half asleep, still in her clothes, something startled her. The silence was broken by a heavy thump. Winnie was unable to tell where the sound came from. It was not uncommon, as some of the ladies might have lingering customers who were willing to pay extra for more time.

There was a series of trashes. Winnie realized the noise was coming from the next room, Candy's room. On and on it went, and then there was loud shouting.

"I told you, before we started!" Candy shouted.

"You are an abomination!" a man's voiced boomed through the wall. "God sees what you are!" he continued.

"That's good," Candy answered. "Maybe, God will tell your wife where you spend your nights."

The next sound was that of Candy screaming in pain.

Winnie jumped from her bed and out into the hall. She heard other doors opening, as others came out of their rooms to investigate.

Thankfully, Candy's room door wasn't locked. Opening the door, Winnie rushed in. Candy was out cold on her bed, her face bloody and bruised. There was a large man standing before the bed, his back to Winnie. He reached into his jacket, pulled out a pistol, aiming it at Candy.

Winnie had no idea what to do, only that she needed to act immediately. She did the first thing that came to her mind.

Near the door, next to Winnie, was a chest of drawers, on it was a hurricane lamp burning a low flame. Winnie took hold of it, tossing it at the man.

It all happened at once. The gun fired, hitting the unconscious Candy directly in the heart, blood spurting across the bed. At that same instance, the lamp broke against the back of the man's head. The kerosene doused his back, and instantly burst into flame. The man screamed, as he bounced from wall to wall, trying to extinguish the fire consuming him.

Just then, Madame Putain rushed into the room. Her first concern was to save the life of one of her customers. An instant such as this could destroy her business. She ran to the man, trying to take hold of him except he was too strong for her. When she did, he bounced around the room, carrying her with him.

Suddenly, Madame Putain's flimsy nightgown caught fire. She released her hold on the man, running about in fear. The man fell onto the bed, the bedsheets immediately were aflame.

The flames from Madame Putain's nightgown flew upward, catching her hair on fire. The screaming woman ran out of the room, toppling over the banister, landing on the floor below.

Winnie left the room. She looked around to see others, standing, watching, in bewilderment. The room was now engulfed in flames. Her survival instincts took hold of her. She dashed down the stairs, jumped over the motionless, burning body of Madame Putain, and ran out the door into the night.

She didn't stop running nor look back. Finally, out of breath, blocks away, she turned for one last look. There was a fire's glow of yellow and orange lighting up the night sky.

Eleven

God's Work

Being owned by Madame Putain, working the Club de Messieurs, was living hell for Winnie, nevertheless it had its benefits. Winnie had never been on her own, her entire life. Now, alone on the streets of New Orleans, she was hungry, tired, and frightened.

She had learned a few things in her time, especially about men, what they want and how to handle them. Only, on the streets, that life was not the way she wanted to go, although, she had her opportunities. She was propositioned by men, both day and night. She turned them all down.

She thought of stealing; only there was nothing to steal. Even if she did take something of value, she wouldn't know where to sell it.

She tried begging, only to be avoided by most, or propositioned by some of the most villainess men.

Many were the days the rains came. She did her best to get out of the downpour, and remain dry. Only, it was not always possible. Often, she would spend the long cold nights sleeping in drenched clothes.

Finally, late one night, as she walked along the harbor past the many taverns, her strength gave way. She felt feverish. The world began spinning, her legs collapsed under her, and she fell to the ground. As she lay in the doorway of a bakery, the smell of bread stirred her. Only, it made her feel weaker, as she fell in and out of consciousness.

Voices, she heard voices, men's voices, laughing, grunting, drunken voices, two or three. Hands on her, all over her, more laughter, someone was lifting her skirt. She felt the chill on her thighs. There were hands on her knees, spreading her legs apart. They were strong men's hands. Then, unexpectedly, the sound of thrashing was all around, as if it all turned into a street brawl.

"Take your hands off of her!" a women's voice shouted. "Get out of here!" There was the sound of more thrashing about.

Winnie felt the hands of the man holding her letting go, his manly weight floating off her. She opened her eyes. The world was a blur. She could only make out the silhouette of a group of people fighting. She strained to clear her sight.

It was three men being fought off by two women. She could no longer keep her eyes open. In the dark behind her eyes, she listened to the battle. In her mind, in her delirium, she pictured it as three demons and two angels fighting for possession of her soul.

When the skirmish stopped, Winnie felt hands on her, again, lifting her up. She strained to open her eyes. Before her was a woman's face, a white woman dressed in black with a bright white halo around her face – truly an angel.

"Have no fear, my child," the woman whispered. That was the last thing Winnie remembered, as she slipped into unconsciousness.

****

Winnie woke to find she was lying on a cot, in what looked to be a small prison cell. Only, there was a crucifix on the wall, and the door was wide open.

She realized she was wearing a clean white nightgown, and someone had washed her, and her hair was clean and combed.

Try as hard as she could, she was not strong enough to sit up.

A woman entered the cell, carrying a tray. It was the women Winnie had seen in her daze, one of the angels, the one who whispered to her.

Now, Winnie realized what she had seen. Women in black with white halos, they were nuns.

"Good, you're awake. You need to eat something, if you're going to regain your strength," the smiling woman said, placing the tray at the foot of the bed. She helped Winnie sit up, and then placed the tray before her. "It's just some clear broth, but it will do you good."

"Where am I? What has happened?" Winnie asked in confusion.

The woman giggled slightly. "You must have many questions." The woman sat down on the edge of the bed. "This is the *Mother of God Mission*. We care for the poor of the city as best we can with food, clothing, and sometimes shelter for those who are ill." The woman placed her hand on Winnie's. "My name is Sister Voleur d'ame. There are two other sisters here, Sister Marie Demone, who you've already met, though I doubt you remember, and lastly, Sister Anne Lutin. We are of the Soeurs de la Misericorde Order in France. What is your name, child?"

"Winnie."

"Well, Winnie, enjoy you broth before it gets cold. I'll be back for the bowl, later."

The woman rose from the bed, standing by the open doorway. Winnie was able to get a good look at her. She realized the connection between what was and what she imagined the night of the brawl.

It was impossible to tell the woman's age, height or even weight. Her loose black habit covered her entire body, save for her hands. The dark opaque veil covered her head so completely, not a strand of hair was visible. Stiff white material covered her neck and framed her face so tightly only an oval of face was seen. It was only possible to say she was a smiling, plain, white woman. Everything else would be guesswork.

Sister Voleur d'ame slowly backed out of the room, continuing to smile. "Have no fear, my child. You are safe, now. Relax, and let the healing hand of God rest upon you."

****

Soon, Winnie was able to eat solid foods. With each day she grew stronger. Eventually, she was able to move around, helping the nuns at the Mother of God Mission. They gave her clean clothes to wear, and allowed her to continue to live with them, sleeping in her cell.

Each day was filled with new excitement. They would start the day early, before sunrise, in prayer. Winnie did not try to hide her disbelief; still, she remained quite throughout, to show respect. She did admit to herself how moved she was by the devotion, faith, and selflessness of these three women.

After morning prayers, they would cook and serve meals for the poor who flood their doorway, everyday. Then they would nurse the ill that they allowed to stay in the few cells. The building was small, which was why it was crowded with the sick and dying. Why they allowed Winnie to have her cell to herself was a mystery.

The mission received a monthly allowance from the local dioceses. Sister Voleur d'ame did everything in her power to put it to good use, however it was never enough. Therefore, time was allotted everyday for begging. The sisters would go to the well-off parts of the city, going from door to door, beseeching for alms. They received pennies, pieces of used clothing, yet often, they were greeted with foul language and doors slammed in their faces. Still, the nuns were never dismayed, they would continue on their mission, always smiling, always giving thanks in prayer.

For these reasons, the battle that once waged war in Winnie's mind began, again. The voices of Jolene and Lucinda were at it. Only, this time the words of Jolene were being backed up by the actions of the sisters of the Soeurs de la Misericorde Order. Winnie began to doubt her life choices, the words of Jolene ringing true, whereas, Lucinda's advice began sounding shallow and pointless.

Late afternoon, the sisters cooked and served supper for twice as many poor as they did in the morning. Winnie worked alongside the sisters. It was a good feeling to be needed, and to live with a purpose.

In the night, one of the sisters remained at the mission watching over the sick and dying, while the other two nuns roamed the streets looking for the needy that were too weak to seek help. Such was the case with Winnie.

Because her strength was still questionable, Winnie was never allowed to go on these late night missions. They ordered her to go to bed early to keep up her health.

Often, Winnie woke in the middle of the night to hear all three nuns gathered in the prayer room, singing hymns of worship.

****

It was obvious the three nuns were not only very much in the moment of each day, and looking toward the future, they had turned their backs on the past. All questions from Winnie about their lives before becoming a nun were ignored, and focus was placed on the present and or the future.

It was the opposite when it came to Winnie. All three sisters seemed interested in Winnie's story. Winnie saw no harm in opening up about her history. She told about her early life on the plantation, her sale to Samuel Runt. All three sisters nearly broke down in tears when she told how the Reverend Lugner betrayed her, foiling her attempt to escape.

"Why would a man of the cloth hand you over to a man like Runt?" Sister Marie Demone asked with dismay.

"For money, he knew Runt would pay handsomely," Winnie explained.

"For money," Sister Voleur d'ame said, sounding surprised. "How much did Runt pay him?"

"I have no idea; I only know it was a large amount."

"Disgraceful," Sister Anne Lutin added.

They went wide-eyed, as she relayed to them her sale to Madame Charbonneau and her education at her school with intent to transform her into a Fancy, a mistress. They lifted their prayers for her, as she told them of the advice she'd received from both Lucinda and Jolene. However, when it came to the telling of her time working the Club de Messieurs, owned by Madame Putain, her shame became too heavy to bear. She lied about that time in her life. She told them she escaped from the school the same night as Jolene. Being young and innocent, Winnie was unable to fend for herself on the cold and cruel streets of New Orleans. She'd fallen on hard times, and became ill.

"And that's when you found me. If not for you three sisters of mercy, I would be dead, right now. I thank God for you," Winnie told them, surprised those words came so easily to her.

"And we thank God for you," Sister Voleur d'ame responded, smiling, as were the other two sisters.

****

"Why do you let me stay?" Winnie asked, one day when it was just the two of them, alone.

"We took you in because you were sick," Sister Voleur d'ame answered.

"But, I'm well, now."

Sister Voleur d'ame smiled gently and shook her head. "No, my dear child, you are not well. You are still sick in your soul. I knew it the moment I laid eyes on you."

A look of shock flushed over Winnie's face. She was speechless, anxious to hear more from this saintly woman.

"God has a plan for you, my dear," Sister Voleur d'ame continued. "I pray you will soon be shown it."

The battle in Winnie's mind was beginning to subside, as the powers of good over evil took hold.

****

A jolt woke Winnie. She felt hands all over her, holding her down. The second she opened her eyes, she saw Sister Voleur d'ame, her face hovering over her, shoving a rag into Winnie's mouth. A gag was then placed around her head to keep the cloth in place, silencing her.

The other two nuns held her in place, and then they ripped off her nightgown. Tearing the material into long strips, they used the strips to tie her to the four corners of the bed. She was now gagged, tied, and naked.

"I'm sorry it has to be this way, my dear child," Sister Voleur d'ame whispered, standing over Winnie. "But, I've prayed about it for days, asking God what part you are to play in all this. We've all sacrificed something. Think of this as a sacrifice, a sacrifice for God. The money we're to make will feed so many of the hungry mouths needing to be fed. You may not understand this now, but you are doing God's work, and you will be blessed for it."

The three nuns left the room, leaving the door open. Winnie heard voices, men's voices. The next moment three sailors entered. Winnie recognized their uniforms. They were sailors in the Confederacy. She'd seen many a young man such as these along the harbor and the backstreets and taverns of New Orleans. Seldom did she see their type in Club de Messieurs. The cost was far out of their range. They drank cheap whiskey and went with only prostitutes they could afford, the elderly, poor, the sickly, and the drug addicts.

"Well, look what we have here," one of them said as all three gleefully inspected her, laughing as they ran their hands over her.

"I'm first," one of them announced.

"Oh no, you're not. I'm the senior officer, here; I go first," said another.

"Senior officer...? You're no officer."

"Well, I'm higher ranked than you two, so, I go first. Now, get out," the first said as he pushed the other two out of the room, closing the door.

He stood over Winnie, smiling at her. "It's been a long time, darlin', you lucky girl."

Twelve

No Justification

It was a nightmare, which Winnie could not wake from. A sea of nameless faces of lust hungry men came and went. They never released her, keeping her naked and tied to her bed, although, they exchanged strips of torn sheet for thick rope. They hand fed her and washed her daily. Even with such care, Winnie was ill, becoming sicker than when she was first brought to the mission.

It was late afternoon, Winnie mentally prepared for the night, except it was becoming more difficult with each passing day. Sister Anne Lutin entered the cell, carrying a tray. On it was a large bowl of hot broth. She sat on the edge of the bed. First, she took the gag out of Winnie's mouth.

"Lift your head up, so I can feed you," the nun commanded.

Holding the bowl in one hand, Sister Anne Lutin carefully spoon-fed Winnie.

"It's scorching hot," Winnie complained.

"Quit your whining. Eat it; it's good for you," the nun grumbled.

Sister Anne Lutin was the eldest of the nuns. Her eyesight and nerves were not what they used to be. With each spoonful, she either missed Winnie's mouth or her hand shook so severely, most of it spilled onto Winnie's chest, burning her.

"Stop wiggling," Sister Anne Lutin ordered.

"It's not me," Winnie insisted, "It's you. At least, untie one of my hands, so I can feed myself. There's not much I can do with only one hand."

Sister Anne Lutin took a long time evaluating the situation. Finally, she placed the bowl on the tray, and slowly untied Winnie's right hand from the bedpost. Taking up the bowl, again, she placed the spoon into Winnie's free hand.

Winnie took a spoonful from the bowl to her mouth, slurping up the broth. She did this three or four times, till she felt the nun's guard was down. Then, with one swift motion, Winnie shoved the bowl of steaming hot broth into Sister Anne Lutin's face.

The old woman toppled off the bed and onto the floor. Surprisingly, she didn't scream, only rolling about on the floor in pain, her hands covering her face, her breathing quick and heavy.

Winnie wasted no time, using her free hand to untie her other hand. Once done, she sat up and quickly untied her feet. When she was free, she jumped off the bed, only to stagger about the room. She had become so weak, she could barely walk.

She found her dress on the floor in the corner of the room, where they had tossed it so long ago.

Sister Anne Lutin was still thrashing about in agony, when suddenly she went still. Her hands fell from her face, exposing the once pink, wrinkled flesh, now, crimson red and creased with burn marks. She had either passed out or the old woman's heart gave out from the strain, and she was dead. Winnie had no time to check, nor did she care.

Winnie ran from the room. She looked about, fearing confronting the other nuns. Passing room after room, she saw the sick and dying the nuns were caring for. A difficult and costly task, nevertheless nothing could justify the wrong they had done to her.

Out of the building, onto the street, she ran, not caring in what direction. She ran till she dropped from exhaustion. Once she got her bearings, she realized she was running to the edge of the city. This was fine with Winnie. Nothing sounded better than to see New Orleans far behind her.

She didn't realize how poorly her health was. She staggered like a drunk, hitting against walls, falling every few steps.

Lying face down in the gutter, she lifted her head to see a familiar sight. Before her was a gate in the center of a high stone wall. Beyond the gate, she could see the mansion. It was Madame Charbonneau's school for Fancy Girls.

Winnie struggled to her feet, staggering to the gate. There were two guards, large men, behind the gate. They looked at her with disgust and no pity.

"I need to speak to Madame Charbonneau," Winnie said, holding desperately onto the bars of the gate.

"Is she expecting you?" asked one of the guards.

"No," Winnie said. "I'm the last person in the world she'd expect to see. But, she'll want to see me. There's money involved."

Just then, she lost all control, the world spun wildly. She lost her grip on the gate, falling unconscious to the ground.

Thirteen

Don't Press Your Luck

A few days later, after they cleaned Winnie, fed her, and nursed her back to health, she stood before Madame Charbonneau in her office.

"We believed you were dead," Madame said. "Not many survived the fire at Club de Messieurs. Where have you been all this time?"

"Surviving," Winnie answered coldly.

"I'm interested to know, why did you come back?" Madame asked.

"I had no place to go. I came on the school by accident. Besides, I have a proposition for you."

"You have a proposition for me?" Charbonneau laughed.

"Yes! When you sold me to Club de Messieurs, it wasn't what I expected, what I was prepared for."

"You went to the highest bidder," Madame insisted.

"Nevertheless, it was not what you trained me to be. Now, I'm willing to be sold again by you, but it has to be to a wealthy gentleman, as was intended."

Madame Charbonneau thought for a moment. "It's a shame you're no longer a virgin," she said in dismay.

"And whose fault is that?" Winnie shot back.

Madame looked at Winnie, astonished. "You're not afraid of me, are you?"

"No, should I be? What can you do to me? I don't believe I'll ever be afraid of anything, again. If anything, you should be afraid of me."

"Me…afraid of you…?"

"There is nothing more dangerous than a person with nothing to lose. And I have nothing to lose. But, I do know what I want. I will work with you anyway you want me to; as long as you sell me in the way I was first promised. If all goes well, we both will profit. If not…well…I told you that I have nothing to lose."

Madame Charbonneau sat down behind her desk. "Very well, we'll play your game. I'll see what I can do. It will take a few days. You may go now." As Winnie made for the door, "Oh, remember, as fearless as you may think you are, I can make you regret you were ever born. Cross me and I will come down on you so harsh, I will have you begging for death, and death will not come."

****

Two day's later; Madame Charbonneau hired a professional photographer, a young man, who hid his age and good looks behind a massive beard, dark and bushy, down to his chest.

He turned the entire parlor into his personal studio. It took nearly the full day for him to get everything the way he wanted it. Finally, one by one, the girls, all the Fancy girls, were prepped, and dressed in one of Charbonneau's most glorious and expensive gowns.

Winnie was the first to be photographed; as she was the reason Charbonneau hired him. He also took the longest time with her. It was only an afterthought of Madame to have the other girls photographed, bringing her business into the modern age.

A week later, Madame Charbonneau received the prints. It was costly; still she felt it was worth it. Normally, when Charbonneau tried to sell one of her girls to a gentleman, she would invite the potential client to dinner. Giving him a chance to meet and assess the young woman in question. This usually worked well, although not in all cases. There were certain wealthy gentlemen who were interested in Madame Charbonneau's services, however, being in the public eye forced them to avoid any connection with her. These were mostly politicians and government officials. Gentlemen whose careers would disappear, if the public knew they had any connection with Madame Charbonneau. Some of them even avoided that part of town, let alone be a guest for dinner.

Madame felt pleased with the results, except for Winnie's photograph. She was very cross with the photographer, giving him what for. She complained so harshly to the photographer, he was forced to return and redo the session in the parlor.

"I realize she may be the lightest skinned Negress that either of us has ever seen. But she is still a Negress. I mean, what the hell do you think we're doing here? We groom black girls for white gentlemen. If they wanted white women, they could search the churches. If they want a woman with experience and know-how, they can prowl the taverns. But if they want a black woman of culture who knows how to please a man, they come to Madame Charbonneau. Now, I want this corrected, or I shall hold back payment."

That was the motivation behind it all – getting paid. The poor young man worked himself into a tizzy. He tried everything, different parts of the room, pull the shades half

58

down. He took shot after shot under different conditions, rushing out to his wagon to develop them.

Finally, late in the evening after a long day, he got the effect Charbonneau hoped for. Actually, the picture was very unlike Winnie, she looked darker than in real life. Nevertheless, that was what Charbonneau paid him for.

He printed a dozen copies. Feeling satisfied, Madame Charbonneau paid him, which pleased the photographer.

The next morning the photos were delivered to potential clients. Not by post, mind you, but hand delivered by Madame's servants. This cut down on any unforeseeable problems, such as nosy interfering wives.

A week passed when Madame Charbonneau summoned Winnie to her office.

"It seems there's been a high offer for you," Madame said with pride, and more than a touch of greed.

"Is he wealthy?" Winnie asked.

"Very, he has more money than God."

"Is he young and handsome?"

"Don't press your luck. No one gets it all in this life."

"Can't you tell me something about him," Winnie pleaded.

"He's from old money, lots of money. He's an eccentric old goat, probably easy to please."

"He's rich and old, is he? Maybe he'll leave everything to me when he dies."

"A mistress doesn't get it all when he dies, the wife does, but if you treat him right, when he dies, he'll leave you a good part of his wealth, despite his wife. My only advice to you is that if you kill him make it look like an accident."

"By the time I'm done with him, he won't know what hit him. This better be the job I've been hoping for, or else."

"And you better be the women he's been hankering for, or else. You came on like a swarm of bees. Better be able to make him happy. Or it's the streets for you. It would seem both of us have been warned. Better do what you're told."

59

Fourteen

Welcome, My Dear

Judge Tordu Malade was a frail old man. As a young man from a wealthy family, he studied law, opening his own law office before the age of twenty. In no time at all, he became one of the top requested lawyers in New Orleans. His fame and fortune was not based on his knowledge and skill, not of the law, that is. His success was due to his conniving. He was a good liar, looking you straight in the eye, winning your confidence and trust. He understood the art of the bribe, the greased palm, and backstabbing.

In only a few years, he bought his way to the top of the judicial system, taking the position of a local judge of New Orleans. He gained the title of *Your Honor*, which he demanded to be called at all time. He spent fifty years on the bench and was still active when Winnie came into his life.

Now in his seventies, Judge Tordu Malade lived alone in a very posh townhouse in the heart of New Orleans. It was walking distance from the courthouse, which he did everyday.

He was always the center of gossip and much speculation. There were only three servants in his employment, a cook, a maid, and a butler. This was considered the bare minimum, if not understaffed, for such a large, luxurious home. He never socialized, turning down invites to dinner parties and the like at the homes of New Orleans's finest, upper crust. His entire life, he never courted any women, so, understandably, he never married. There were rumors of weekly visits by local prostitutes, even in his seventies. The report from these women, although they would never give details, was that Judge Tordu Malade had many strange sexual appetites, making marriage impossible and socializing with workingwomen a must. Although, Malade decided this would all change, if only he could find the one woman who could fulfill all his lustful bizarre tastes.

A cab was hired to take Winnie to the home of Judge Malade. The butler, a pasty faced white man of undistinguishable age, dressed in black, answered the door. The cabbie was instructed to bring in Winnie's suitcase and place it on the floor at the foot of the stairs. To her surprise, there were other suitcases there.

Once alone, the butler pointed to two large sliding pocket doors. "Please, follow me," he stated coldly, sounding disinterested. He motioned for her to enter. "You can wait here with the others." Winnie entered; he slid the doors closed behind her.

It was a large parlor, filled with fineries. Yet, Winnie took notice of none of it. What caught her eye was the five women that sat about the room, waiting. They were all young, beautiful, delicately dressed, and black. Winnie assumed they were all Fancy Girls, like herself.

They all half-smiled and nodded to her, and she to them. There was strangeness in the air that made it awkward to speak with one another. So, Winnie took a seat, and waited in silence with the others.

A few minutes later, the pocket doors slide opened, the butler entered.

"My name is Nez Marron. I work for Judge Tordu Malade. I want to congratulate each of you on making it through the first part of being selected."

As Nez spoke, Winnie realized that her sale to the judge was not as solid as Madame Charbonneau led her to believe. This explained the other girls, and their luggage in the foyer. Judge Malade would be selecting only one for the position. The ones rejected, would immediately be sent back to where they came. Although, the arrangement was filled with uncertainty, Winnie was determined to be the one chosen. She dreaded going back to Madame Charbonneau's.

Nez continued, "One by one, each in turn will enter the next room." He pointed to a door at the far end of the parlor. "The judge will interview all of you, but only one will be selected. Speak only when spoken to, and always address him as *Your Honor*. You will be first," he ordered, pointing at one of the young women.

She sat up, wide-eyed, as if Nez had pointed a gun at her, firing, and just barely missing her. She rose, and walked to the door. Nez opened the door, pushed her inside, slamming it behind her.

A long moment of silence passed, and then shouts from the old man thundered through the door.

"Nez, get this worthless animal out of my sight," were the only words they all heard clearly.

A few minutes later, there was a ruckus in the hall. It was obvious the girl had been rejected. A cabbie was carrying her luggage out the front door to the cab that would take her back to where she came.

One by one, they were summoned to the next room, only to be rejected with shouts of anger from the old man. Each time was followed by the sound of luggage being carted and a carriage whisking the poor girl away.

Call it good fortune or misfortune, for whatever reason, Winnie was to be last. She sat in the parlor, alone, trying to imaging what she would say and do once confronted by the judge. What had the other girls done wrong?

Finally, it was her turn. Nez walked her to the door, opened it, and shoved her within. The room was dark, save for a single candle burning dull on a desk. The judge did not sit behind the desk, but in a chair to one side.

"Come closer. Let me see you," the old man's voice cracked like dry winter leaves underfoot.

As she approached, she was able to make out his features. She stood before this ancient creature, trying not to show the fear that ran up and down her spine. He sat in the chair like a vulture on a fence, hunched over, his long neck covered in sagging flesh. His face was wrinkled as if windblown. His nose was large, protruding downward like the beak of a scavenger. One look at him made a person doubtful that he was capable of any of the sexual activity that he was known for.

He lifted the candle from off the desk, shining the light to get a better look at her.

"You're a pretty little thing, I'll give you that much," he stated. A look of disappointment appeared on his face. "A bit light-skinned are you? You look more white than dark. You wouldn't try to be passing off as a black girl, now, would you?"

"Why would anyone want to pass as black, in this day and age?" she replied, gently, yet firm.

He laughed, "You speak as if there will be a day when it won't matter. You're sassy; I like that. What is your name, child."

"They call me Winnie, Your Honor."

"And I understand you're experienced beyond your years, so I've been told by your Madame."

"Yes, I am, Your Honor."

"Do you know why I rejected those other girls?"

"I'm afraid I don't, Your Honor."

"They were sent here by their Madame, just like you. Said to be experienced. But what they don't comprehend is a true gentleman of quality has tastes for the unusual, not the mundane. I need a woman with an open mind to help me along on my adventures. Not one who finds them hard to comprehend or giggles throughout. I need a real woman, a mature woman. Are you that kind of woman, Winnie?"

"Yes I am, Your Honor. I'm not afraid to try anything new, or do what I'm told. Because I don't care, I want to succeed for the pleasure of succeeding. If making you happy, furthers my happiness, then so be it. I will do anything you ask of me. If you want to make love to me while I strangle you to death, I will. Name your dream and I will make it true."

"That's the kind of talk I like," he said, placing the candle back on the desk. "Now, for the test the others could not pass."

"Name it, Your Honor."

"I want you to slap me...hard!" he commanded.

Without a moment hesitation, Winnie gave him the back of her hand, and for good measure, brought her hand around, giving him another slap, harder than the first.

His head fell back, against the top of his chair. There was a strange look of contentment on his face, almost blissful.

"Spit on me," he ordered in a hazy bliss.

She did just that, the spittle dripping from under his eye to his lips.

Afraid he'd lost consciousness, she reached out to him. Before she could touch him, he mumbled soft and low.

"Tell Nez to take you and your luggage to your new room. Welcome, my dear."

Fifteen

Utterly Alone

Weeks passed, Winnie spent her days in solitude. She never left the house; though she was free to enter every room, save for the library and the judge's bedroom. Each day, she had some contact with Nez the butler, mostly one or two sentences concerning conduct and house rules. He never answered any of her questions, directly that is.

The maid was a petite young black girl by the name of Blesses who just came up to Winnie's chin. She moved about the house like a silent storm, constantly cleaning, doing laundry, making beds, never taking time to speak to anyone. When Winnie confronted her, she would bow her head, never looking her in the eyes, answering with the least amount of words needed to convey the thought. At first, Winnie took it to be shyness. Except in time Winnie sensed it was more of fear, like a dog that had been beaten into submission, afraid every moment of doing wrong, of another beating.

She called herself *Ma Cherie*. She was the complete ruler of her domain, the queen of the kitchen. She did all the cooking for the entire household. Three meals served each day, with two menus, one for the workers, and a separate finer meal for Judge Malade. Although the two menus were similar, as the help were treated well, at least when it came to food, besides the judge was not a picky eater. Winnie was served the same as the judge, the finer food, although she always dined alone.

Ma Cherie never sat down to a meal. She existed on small tastes of her own cooking throughout the day. Because of this, now a middle-aged black woman, she remained the same weight as when she was a young girl.

Though never rude, yet always short, Ma Cherie was usually too busy for idle chitchat.

Only, the weeks of being alone weighted heavily on Winnie. In all that time, she never once laid eyes on the judge. Nez only spoke to her to give orders, always looking down his nose at her. Blesses was too frightened to be approached. The home library on the first floor was off limits, so no books to read. There are many hours in a day, hours made longer by isolation. Ma Cherie was Winnie's only hope of remaining sane.

"Hand me that slotted spoon," Ma Cherie said, pointing to a long spoon laying on the kitchen table, when Winnie entered the room.

"You mean this one, here?"

"That's the one, sweetie." Ma Cherie took hold of the spoon, stirring the contents of the pot. "So, what can I do for ya, missy?"

Winnie figured if they were to have a conversation, it would be on Ma Cherie's terms. "I don't know, I just came in to see if I could help."

"Can ya cook, child?"

"No, not really, but I'm not afraid to learn."

Ma Cherie gave Winnie the strangest of looks. Putting the lid on the pot, she moved to the table. "Can ya cut onions?"

"I guess so," Winnie answered as the old woman handed her a long knife, pointing to a sack of onions on the floor.

Winnie made a start of it, trying her best, yet unsure of herself.

Ma Cherie smiled, speaking to Winnie softly in a motherly fashion. "No, no, honey. Not on the table, on the cutting board. And ya hold the knife like this. Keep ya fingers curled, so ya don't cut 'em. Move like this, don't work the knife, let the knife work for y'all."

In time, Winnie got the hang of it. After three onions successfully cut and sliced, she felt confident enough to ask questions.

"So, how long have you worked for the judge?" Winnie asked casually.

Ma Cherie's smile returned. "Ya lonesome, ain't ya?"

Winnie looked back in surprise.

"I can see it in ya face," the old woman chuckled.

"Is it that noticeable?"

"Listen to me, girl," Ma Cherie continued. "Ya a pretty young thing, ya need to get yourself out of this place as soon as ya can. Run away as fast as ya can."

"I don't understand," Winnie said.

"This is a bad place ya wound up in. This is a house of evil. Ain't no good gonna come ya way, livin' here."

"Why haven't you run away? You're still here," Winnie pointed out.

"I'm just the cook, child. As long as I don't burn anything, nobody gonna pay any attention to me. I got it easy. It's a good life. But child, y'all are the judge's plaything. And he's an evil man. Ya need to get out of here before ya lose ya life, or worse, ya lose ya soul."

"I don't believe such nonsense," Winnie countered. "I can take care of myself. I know what side the bread is buttered. I'll get out of here someday, but on my own terms. One day, I'll be a rich woman, and have a house twice as big as this one."

"Girl, ya sound just like me when I was your age. There weren't nobody could teach me nothin' because I knew it all, only ya got it all wrong. Yeah, ya might survive this place, and strike it rich someday. Except, when ya dead and gone ya don't take nothin' with ya but ya soul."

"I told you, I don't believe those types of things," Winnie protested.

"Oh, ya don't have to believe in them for them to happen, anyways. As long as there's life there's hope. As long as there's breath in the body, God's listenin'."

"I don't believe in God, either," Winnie added.

A look of shock came over Ma Cherie. "Ya don't believe in God? What else is there to believe in?"

"Yourself…!" Winnie demanded.

"Ya foolish, foolish girl, ya can't wish these things away. There is a God, there is a heaven and hell, they don't just stop being because ya don't believe in 'em."

Ma Cherie took hold of Winnie. The old woman looked up, her eyes wide, as if the ceiling flew away and she was looking to heaven. "Dear Lord, have mercy on this young foolish child who ain't got a lick of sense in her head."

"Let go of me, you old fool," Winnie shouted, trying to break free of Ma Cherie's grip.

"Let's get down on our knees, right now, child. It ain't too late."

"Silly old crow," Winnie said as she broke free, pushing Ma Cherie from her. She rushed out of the kitchen. As she ran up the stairs, she could still hear the old woman raving.

"The demons are gonna get ya. Don't worry, child, I'll pray for ya. It ain't too late, child!"

At the top of the stairs, Winnie ran into her room, as if the devil himself were after her. After slamming her bedroom door shut, she locked it, and ran to her bed.

The voices started in her head, once more. This time it was more than the usual two voices of Jolene and Lucinda. Now there was a third voice, that of Ma Cherie.

"Quiet!" she shouted. The voices disappeared. She was alone, utterly alone.

Sixteen

The Hanging Judge

Anticipation hung heavy over Winnie's head, like the sword of Damocles, an ever-present and imminent danger. She knew why she was there. She also knew even at his age, Judge Tordu Malade felt as randy as a younger man. As well, she knew his appetite in such matters was bizarre, to say the least. She could only hope it was something she could at least tolerate.

Like so many of the elderly, Judge Malade enjoyed a structured life, seldom varying from his daily routine. His servant, Nez, would wake him each day one hour before sunrise. And then, help him prepare for the day, shaving him, combing his hair, and helping him select his clothes and get dressed. The judge bathed only once every six months. Judge Malade was old school, believing more than two baths per year was detrimental to one's health.

Ma Cherie was perfectly willing to get up early enough to cook a breakfast for the judge, except, the city included two meals each day along with his salary. He'd wait to eat breakfast when he arrived at his office, which always consisted of a soft-boiled egg, bread, and a cup of strong tea.

Less than a quarter mile from the courthouse, the judge enjoyed his early walks alone to his office, taking pleasure in the brisk morning air, the sunlight now bringing light to the world.

At his office, he would go over his schedule for the day, as he sipped his tea. Ten minutes before his first hearing in the morning, he would put on his long black robe. This is when the strangeness started. Before putting on his robe, he would remove all his clothes, folding them into a neat pile. When he entered the courtroom, wearing his judge's robe, no one was aware he was naked underneath. This was only an offshoot of his perversion.

Judge Tordu Malade was known as the *Hanging Judge*. The wealthy gladly paid a fee not to appear in his court, and it was only the rich who could afford to do so. Talk was he seemingly took pleasure in handing down overly strong and cruel sentences. Little did they know how true this was, or how much pleasure he truly derived from showering people with misery, pain, and most of all death.

If the crime called for a thirty-day jail sentence, he would sentence them to ninety-days. A year became five; ten became twenty or a life sentence. Even when evidence was slim to none against the accused, the penalty was overly harsh. What was worst of all, and gave the judge the most pleasure, was condemning the accused to death. Hanging was the most common form of execution, though death by firing squad was not unheard of.

The pleasures Judge Malade received were numerous. The surge of power, the power over life and death, the narcissism of playing God, brought him to bliss. However, the greatest delight he experienced from sending someone to the gallows cannot be explained in civil terms. Just say that being naked under his robe played a major part of this ecstasy. He would often fall into a swoon, retiring to his office for an hour or more to collect himself, to continue the day.

So went each day for Judge Tordu Malade, returning in the evening, entering his home through the backdoor, avoiding contact with anyone, except Nez. The judge would take his meals in his room, reading late into the evening. He was strongly addicted to morphine and codeine, which he would partake of each night before going to bed.

His work schedule finished early on Fridays, leaving his weekends free, mostly spending his time locked in his room. Though it was the talk there were certain times when a woman of the streets was hired. When word among such women circulated, warning one another of his monstrous ways, no woman would visit at any price. This was the reason Winnie was purchased.

As hideous and grotesque as this all appeared, it is only the outer shell of his atrocities. Winnie had no idea what lay in wait for her; however, she was soon to find out.

Chapter Seventeen

Guilty

It was a Saturday night; Winnie was in her room, on her bed, fully dressed. The knock on the door shocked her to her feet. It opened slowly; Nez stood in the doorway.

"The judge wants you. Follow me," was all he said, turning and walking away. He said this in a manner that did not require or expect a response, only to follow him, which Winnie did.

They walked down the stairs. On the first floor, they went to a door at the back, under the stairs. Of course, Winnie noticed the door before, except whenever she tried it, she found it locked. Nez opened the door. Taking a lamp from a table below a wall mirror, he entered, walking down the stairs.

"Follow me," he repeated; Winnie complied.

It was dark at the bottom of the stairs. Winnie kept her eyes fixed on the light of the lamp before her, or surely she would have lost her way.

They passed through a doorway into a well-lit room with lamps along the walls. Winnie was taken aback by what she saw. Though a bit smaller, the room was an exact replica of a courtroom, except in front of the judge's bench was a gallows. There was no platform to the gallows, just a trapdoor.

Seated at the judge's podium was Judge Malade, clad in his black robe, gavel in hand. Nez guided Winnie before the bench. There he bound her hands behind her back. He placed her over the trapdoor under the hangman's noose.

"What are you doing?" Winnie protested.

Judge Malade hammered his gavel onto the bench. "Silence in the court...silence in the court. The accused will remain silent; only speak when you are spoken to. You will have your turn to make your defense. Silence in the court!"

Winnie fought back, as Nez bound her feet together, except he was too strong for her to resist. He placed the noose over her head, tightening it around her neck.

Judge Malade hit his gavel down. "Will the prosecutor explain to the court what this woman is accused of; what are her crimes?"

Nez stepped forward. "Your Honor, she is accused of assault and battery. She did strike and spit on one Judge Tordu Malade."

"You told me to do those things!" Winnie shouted in her defense.

"Silence...silence," the judge shouted back, pounding his gavel down.

"The prosecution rests," Nez proclaimed, walking away, leaving the room.

Judge Malade looked down from his bench. "So, young lady, do you understand what crimes you are accused of? What do you have to say for yourself?"

Winnie wanted to scream; only she knew she needed to stay calm. "You were the one who told me to do it."

"Now, why would I do such a thing?" the judge argued.

Winnie's mind was a whirl. She knew there was nothing she could say that would be of any benefit. She struggled with her bonds; her eyes searching the room for something, anything.

Judge Malade shouted down at her from the bench. "Your crimes are horrific! Normally, punishment would be a prison sentence. Except, this crime was committed against a city official, making the crime more heinous, demanding a greater penalty. The court has taken every aspect of this case, and we have come to only one possible solution. For the assault and battering of a city official, the court sentences you to be hanged by the neck until you are dead, and may God have mercy on your soul."

Just then, Judge Malade reached across his podium, pulling a leaver, releasing the trapdoor that Winnie stood upon.

"No...!" she shouted, just as she went sailing down into the darkness below. As she fell, she mentally waited for the rope to go taunt, snapping her neck. Instead, there was a quick light pull, as the rope snapped. She flew down into the darkness.

An instant later, she landed in something wet and soft. It was too dark to see where she was. Someone held a lamp, exposing only their outline. Then she recognized it was Nez smiling at her. She looked about. She had landed in a pigsty with three large pigs grunting in her face.

She jumped to her feet, covered in mud, slop, and feces.

"What is this, some kind of sick joke?" she shouted at Nez.

"Oh, no, this is no joke," he said solemnly, the smile leaving his face. "You'll do this many times, but one day the rope will be real, and you will be dead. You'll never know when."

Meanwhile, Judge Tordu Malade fell out of his chair, and lie on the floor, overcome with ecstasy.

Eighteen

Against Nature

This had become Winnie's life, seated on the edge of the world, waiting for the moment to be pushed into the abyss. It was not a comfortable place to live.

The powers that be, understood her pain. This was why security was trebled. Winnie couldn't as much as look out a window without seeing a guard on the other side of the glass.

There was nowhere or no one Winnie could turn to. Nez never spoke with her; Blesses was too frightened to talk with her. As for Ma Cherie, Winnie refused to speak with her, not wanting to go down that road, again.

Twice each month, Winnie went through the ordeal of the mock court in the basement. Each time was the same. Winnie was escorted to the trial from her room to the basement by Nez who had taken to holding her at gunpoint. There would be no disobedience from her with a pistol pressed into her ribs.

Each time Winnie went through this nightmare, it became more torturous. She could never be sure if the gallows' rope would break and she would drop to the pigsty below or not. Nez warned her that one day her hanging would be real. She held no way of knowing how long her luck would hold out, except it was only a matter of time.

It had been three weeks since the last basement trial. Nez came to Winnie's room to collect her. All throughout the long walk to the chamber, he kept his pistol pressed against her back.

Below, in the courtroom, Judge Malade waited, seated at the bench, and dressed in his long black robe.

Since using a pistol, Nez varied from his usual procedure. He would first place Winnie over the trapdoor, and then place the noose over her head. At that point, he would tuck the pistol in his belt. Now, with both hands free, he would tighten the noose around her neck, and then go behind her to tie her hands and feet. Once this was all done, the trial could commence, with Nez playing the part of the prosecutor.

For the past three weeks, Winnie played the same scenario in her mind, over and over, again. She knew what she had to do, and when to do it.

As soon as Nez placed the noose over her head and tucked his pistol in his belt, Winnie reached out, grabbing the gun, shooting Nez in the gut. There was a big puff of smoke from the gunshot, Nez went flying backwards, landing on the floor before the bench.

Seeing what just happened, not wanting to take any risk, Judge Malade reached over, pulling the trapdoor leaver. With her hands and legs not bound, Winnie spread her legs apart, just as the trapdoor fell. This prevented her from falling. She could see the darkness, and smell the pigs, below.

Always prepared for the worst, Judge Malade picked up a pistol off his desk, pointing it at Winnie, only he was too slow. Winnie pulled off a shot, hitting Judge Malade in the forehead. The blast slammed him backwards, landing, chair and all, onto the floor.

As carefully as she could, Winnie moved away from the opening at her feet. Removing the noose from her neck, just for the sake of curiosity, she tugged hard on the rope. It held. If she hadn't acted, she would be dead.

Thankfully, the mock courtroom was soundproof, Judge Malade had seen to that. No one would come to investigate.

Winnie knew she had to escape, she also knew what she was up against, the guards outside. Only, now she was armed.

****

Winnie put as many clothes on as she could without it being noticeable. She also put on as much jewelry as she could without being obvious. She ransacked the judge's bedroom. Not surprisingly, she found nothing of any value, except for twenty dollars in coins under his mattress.

When she felt as prepared as she could be, she swung open the front door. Immediately, the guards in the front of the house rushed toward her.

"Help...help...!" she shouted in terror. "Quick! Someone has shot His Honor!" she told them, as they ran up the front stairs. She made such a fuss, the guard from the back of the house came running around.

They all took out their guns. The first guard up the stairs looked to her. "Where is he?"

"In the basement...quick...I don't know if he's breathing!"

They all ran passed her and into the house. Although they were hired to keep those outside from coming in, and to keep those within from getting out, the safety of Judge Tordu Malade was paramount. They rushed through the house to the basement door, and then down.

72

Winnie couldn't believe her good fortune. All the time, her hand was in her pocket with firm grip on the pistol. She was thankful she didn't have to use it. Hopefully, she would never need it.

She ran down the front stairs to the street, never looking back. She needed to lose herself in the city. Once the guards put two and two together, they would be after her.

****

Winnie figured they would be looking for her, once the smoke settled. The wise thing to do was to head out of town. She knew they would assume she'd do just that, which was why she did the opposite, heading for the harbor.

She'd learned her lesson well from the last time she was living on the streets. She vowed not to make the same mistakes. This time would be different. She had better judgment and resolve in her belief, or rather lack there of. As well, this time she had twenty dollars and a gun.

It was late in the night, even for the taverns along the harbor, some were closed. As she passed by *The Black Swan Tavern* she looked through the window. There were few customers, most of them too drunk to get out of their chairs. In the corner of the room, five men sat around a circular table, playing cards. There was only one bartender on duty.

Winnie entered, immediately walking up to the bar. No one paid her any attention.

"Can I get something to eat?" she asked the man behind the bar.

"Kitchen's closed, but if ya buy somethin' to drink, I can give some buttered bread."

Winnie stood at the bar drinking her rum and eating her buttered bread, she turned, eyeing the card game in progress. Of the five men seated at the table, it was obvious four of them were sailors, but not the fifth. He was visibly a white southern gentleman, although a bit rough around the edges, clearly from hard travel and lack of sleep. His striking good looks captivated Winnie who was having a difficult time trying not to look at him. Finally, she tried not to make her staring look so obvious. It was too late, he noticed her. He smiled at her; it went straight to her heart, melting her from the inside out.

He sat with his back to the wall, clearly winning almost every hand, to the chagrin of the other four.

The sailor with his back to Winnie, a baldheaded fellow, seated across from the handsome man, pulled out his pistol.

"I don't know what just happened, and I don't know how you did it, but I'd say we were cheated," the man grunted.

The handsome man didn't seem put-off in the slightest by a gun being pointed at him. "It's just skill, my friend, unadulterated skill."

"Well, I say you cheated. Just push those winnings this aways."

"I'm afraid I can't do that, friend," the handsome man said sternly.

"Then I'm just gonna have to take it."

"Over my dead body…"

"That could be arranged," the bald headed man said laughingly as he pulled the gun's hammer back.

It was a feeling, not something she could put into words. It was like moving about in a dream. Winnie unconsciously knew what she had to do, so she did it, only, not knowing the reason why. She walked over to the table, pulled out her gun, and placed it hard against the back of the baldheaded man's head.

Feeling cold steel on his skin, he instinctively knew what to do. He clicked the hammer back into place, and laid his gun down on the table.

"Thank you, darling," the handsome man said, smiling at Winnie. This time she felt no shyness and smiled back. "Well, gentleman, it's been an exciting and interesting evening, but I'm afraid we must be going," he said, shoveling the money across the table to him, and into his travel bag slung over his shoulder.

Rising from his chair, he carefully moved from the table to stand next to Winnie.

"Come, my dear. I suspect these gentlemen would like to be alone for awhile to lick their wounds."

They backed up slowly, always keeping aim. As they moved past the bar, the bartender smiled and nodded, giving his unspoken approval.

"Oh, what the hell…" the handsome man stated. "We've gone this far, we might as well go all the way." After taking his pistol out of his travel bag, he pointed it at the bartender, wiping the smug smile off his face. "Let's have it. Give us all your money."

Reluctantly, the bartender handed over the till. The handsome man placed it in his travel bag.

Just as they were leaving the tavern, the handsome man made one last proclamation, "One last thing. I want all of you to count to one hundred, before leaving. I may just have a mind to stand outside and do the same. I'll shoot the first man that leaves before then."

With that, they stood outside the Black Swan, the handsome man smiled one last time through the window at some very sour looking faces.

"Shall we, my dear," he said.

The two of them ran off laughing down along the harbor.

"Not bad for one night," the handsome man remarked as he emptied the cash in his travel bag onto the bed.

It was a small, dank, one-room apartment over *The Tin Angel Tavern*, a mile down from The Black Swan.

Without counting, he split the money into two takes. "This is your half," he stated, pointing to the half farthest from him. Winnie didn't react, she just looked at him. Finally, when she was about to take her share, he leaned across the bed, placing his hand on hers. "We make a good team. This is nothing compared to what we could make, if we work together."

"I'm not a criminal," Winnie said, still smiling, trying to keep it friendly.

"Of course, you're not," he laughed. "No one is born that way, to be exact; it's something you must acquire. Not a criminal? You could have fooled me. Now, I can tell you're a true libertine. You're someone who knows what they want, and won't let superstitious ideas of right and wrong stop them. If anyone has what you want, you take it. They get in the way, you eliminate them. But there is such a thing as honor among thieves. There comes a time when you need to trust somebody, and it might as well be me."

Winnie was about to pickup her share, and then left it. "So, what do you have in mind?" she asked.

"Some gambling, which I'm good at, thievery, murder, whatever it takes. A libertine knows a libertine when they see one of their own."

"And what is a libertine?" Winnie asked.

"A nonconformist, being their own god, they bow a knee to no one."

"What about morals?" she asked.

"What about it? A libertine can be moral. We are moral to nature, the true queen of us all. That which goes against nature is sin, everything else is blasphemy, and libertines always obey nature."

"And how is that?"

"Nature is the law. We are born this way, to be who we are, and follow our own wants and destiny. But, mankind wants to control us all, so, they invent things, such as God, using words like: crime and sin. The only crime and sin we commit is when we go against our nature. A tribe on a South Pacific island thinks one way, and the citizens of Paris think another. Who's to say which is right?

"All actions, in themselves, are neither good nor bad. It is man who labels these actions, committing the true sin of going against nature.

"That slight murmur you hear in your brain protesting against what the world calls *wickedness* is nothing more than the prejudices that have been forced into you, by others.

"That feeling of remorse, or sentiment, of guilt is only what impressions we receive as a child, drilled into us by the church, the schools, and the government. And these ideas of theirs keep changing, whereas, nature remains consistent. There is no crime or sin, other than not following your nature. Live for yourself, as your nature dictates. You and you alone are god."

His speech left her breathless, her mind reeling. He gathered the money in a wad, stashing it in a drawer in the nightstand by the bed.

He continued, "So, what do you say? Shall we throw in our lots together? I can see this will be a very prosperous coalition."

"We'll see. I'll give it a try and see how it goes," Winnie answered, thinking it the wise choice.

"Now, let's get undress and go to bed," he said, turning down the bedsheets.

"Whoa!" she protested. "A partnership is one thing, I didn't agree to anything more."

He straightened up, and turned to her. "What do you want to do, sleep on the floor? This is my bed; I'm willing to share it with you. I can't believe after all I've just said, you continue to be a criminal against your own nature. The second our eyes met, I knew I wanted you, and that you wanted me. Don't be so bourgeois,"

"But, I don't even know your name; my name is Winnie."

"Graham…Graham Dorsey. Now, undress and get in bed."

Chapter Nineteen

The Chicken and the Fox

Life with Graham Dorsey quickly became a whirlwind. There was much good about it as well as bad, and sadly, Winnie foolishly could not distinguish one from the other.

It is safe to say Winnie fell deeply in love with Graham Dorsey. It was easy to do. He was everything she'd ever wanted in a man, and more, or so it would appear.

Besides his good-looks, he was a true gentleman with a charisma that attracted people to him. He was attentive to Winnie, both as a partner and a lover, always treating her like a queen, which made her reciprocate, placing him high above herself.

True, he was a scallywag, she could not deny it. Except, she had bought into his logic and philosophy of life, completely, overlooking his social and moral shortcomings. In fact, it became one of the reasons she was so attracted to him. Her man wasn't like the others. He didn't keep normal hours, or work a normal job. He was industrious, always trying to better their lives. He didn't wait for things to happen, he made them happen. She idolized him, and was proud to be a part of his plans.

Their crimes were many and daily; nothing was too big or too small. They burgled homes, Winnie keeping watch. There were late night card games with Winnie seated behind the other players, giving Graham signals. This didn't always work. Often, they would have to shoot their way out, after being caught cheating. After the taverns closed, late at night, there were always drunks to roll. Mostly sailors along the harbor on their way back to their ships.

Winnie no longer heard the arguing of Jolene and Lucinda in her mind. She gave it up when she teamed with Graham. Although, secretly, she was glad they never committed a murder, knowing Graham was perfectly willing and able to do so, if need be. Why she felt this way was beyond her. It went against her new beliefs. After all, there is no such thing as sin, and a crime is a crime, one no greater than the other. Still, she felt pleased it never came down to it.

Though words were never spoken, it was clear to see Winnie was head over heels in love with Graham Dorsey. She followed him around like a pup. Whatever he said was law. She was always trying to please him. She trusted him fully. Only he handled the money, although she never wanted for anything.

In time, they moved from his dilapidated one-room to an apartment far from the harbor. By the way they dressed and lived, for all purposes; people would suspect them of being honest, middle-class citizens.

They lived well, only eating at the finest restaurants, wearing the finest clothing. In time, connecting with some of the upper crust of New Orleans, they moved from middle-class to upper. Everyone who was anyone knew them. They were invited to the finest homes for supper parties and galas. Eventually, they were considered the uppity-ups they spent time with.

With their new position in life came new opportunities. All crimes had ceased, except cheating at gambling. These new gamblers were gentlemen of substance. A night of winning at cards was far more lucrative than a month of home burglaries and rolling drunks.

However, Winnie signaling what the other players' hands were was not going to work. In the old days, if they were caught, they'd reach for their guns and fight their way out. Now, there was more to be lost, if they were found out. Word would get around and they'd be black listed from high society, never to return.

It was Graham's fine criminal mind that came up with a solution. All card games would be at Graham's apartment. This was easy to accomplish, as most of the men attending these games where married. Their wives did not enjoy having to host these gatherings, nor did the men cherish the idea of the expense of renting a space at a club or tavern. Besides, Graham was a gracious host. Food and libations were always served. This is where Winnie and the con came in.

Winnie would prepare and serve food to the players, as well as all the liquor they could want. All portions were small, purposely to have Winnie hovering over the game table. She'd be finely dressed, wearing a necklace from which dangled a large ruby. The backing of the ruby was like a mirror. So, as Winnie served around the table, Graham was able to see the reflection of the other's hands in the ruby. No one ever caught on.

Strangely enough, those who lost to Graham were only more determined to beat him. They would come back again and again. When word about his winning skills circled the city, instead of deterring, it brought even more players. Eventually, getting a seat at one of Graham Dorsey's card games became nearly impossible without making reservations weeks in advance.

"I have a surprise for you," Graham said as he reached out his hand to help Winnie into the carriage.

As they rode through the streets of New Orleans, Winnie could only wonder what Graham was up to. When they entered the better part of the city, she could only imagine they were going to a dinner party at the home of one of their wealthy friends.

When they halted in front of a three-story townhouse, Graham helped Winnie out of the carriage. Winnie looked the building up and down. Not recognizing the building, she could only suspect they were to visit someone they never had before.

"So, what do you think?" Graham asked, figuratively running his hand along the building from top to bottom. "I bought it yesterday," he concluded.

Winnie burst into laughter. "It's beautiful, but can we afford it?"

A solemn look took over Graham. "*I* bought it yesterday," he repeated, emphasizing the word *I*, clearly distort over Winnie using the word *we*. Sure, she played a part in their success, yet only a small part. It was his genius that got them where they were, and he was not going to share in that.

When they entered the building, Winnie was surprised to find that Graham already furnished the home from top to bottom. The first floor was a circular layout of a large parlor, a reading room, a dining room, and a kitchen.

The second floor was a line of six bedrooms, all of good size, and decorated in the finest money could buy.

The third floor was the most surprising. It was one large room, an apartment to itself. It was a combination bedroom, library, reading room and parlor, as well as an area for card playing with a well stocked bar.

"This is where we will spend most of our time, my dear," Graham said, walking to one of the many floor-to-ceiling windows on the far wall.

Winnie walked over to stand by Graham, looking out the window, on the street below.

"If this is our room, what will you do with all those bedrooms on the second floor?" she asked.

"I was thinking," he replied. "We should make good money with the card games. And what they don't gamble away, they surely will spend on a Fancy. What Southern gentleman doesn't enjoy time with a well-trained colored girl? Just like you, my dear."

Winnie shot Graham a questioning look.

"How long did you think you could keep that from me?" he laughed, walking from the window to the bar, to pour them both a drink. "The chicken can never outfox the fox."

Twenty

Hypocrite

Life was good…for a time. Everything was going the way Graham predicted. Nearly every night, a card game was held on the third floor. Winnie would serve drinks and sandwiches. Wearing her mirrored gem around her neck, Graham always knew everyone's hand. He purposely lost the smaller hands, to keep away suspicion. They were making money hand over fist.

It was the day Graham brought three Fancy Girls home to work the bedrooms on the second floor that things began to change. They were three young dark-skinned beauties. Winnie disliked them from the start. Sensing this, the three kept out of Winnie's way. To be blunt and honest, Winnie was jealous of Graham's attention to them. He never slept with any of them, only with her; still, she knew the temptation. She feared it would only be a matter of time.

Now with the girls, they were doubling their weekly take. What they didn't lose at the gambling table, they spent on the Fancies. Every gentleman left at the end of the night with empty pockets.

For weeks, Winnie never left their home without Graham at her side. The premonition in her mind played over and over. Finally, when she realized that was no way to live, she hired a cab for a day of shopping. She tried her best to put it out of her mind, only, the entire day it haunted her. Jealousy is the green demon that consumes like fire.

It was late afternoon when Winnie returned home, all was quiet. The kitchen staff was busy preparing dinner. They hardly noticed Winnie when she entered.

When she found no one in the parlor, she rushed to the third floor, ignoring the second floor as best she could, as she ran up the stairs.

Entering the third floor apartment, she spun around in all directions. Graham was not there. This left her with only two possibilities and three options. Either Graham was out, and all she could do was to sit and wait, or he was on the second floor. Again, she could sit and wait, or she could go to the second floor and investigate.

She tiptoed down the stairs, standing quietly on the second floor landing, listening. There was no sound. Then she heard it. What she feared the most and suspected to hear, the sound of lovers in the bedroom at the end of the hall.

The door was unlocked. Winnie swung the door open, and entered. There was Graham, naked on the bed, one of the new Fancy Girls, naked as well, in his arms.

By the way he slurred his words; it was obvious he was drunk. "Winnie, my dear, come in and join us," he laughed, dismissing his actions.

As far as Winnie was concerned, he couldn't have said harsher words. She rushed out of the room, up the stairs to the apartment.

On the third floor, Winnie went straight to the dresser drawer where they kept the gambling money. Graham entered, standing in the center of the room, fully naked.

"What the hell do you think you're doing?" he shouted.

"I'm taking my share of the money, and I'm leaving," she shouted back.

She held the cash up to him. She split the wad in half, putting one half in her pocket, the other half she threw into his face.

"I don't understand you. What's this all about?" he questioned as she walked passed him.

"I thought we had something special together. I guess I was wrong," she said, walking out of the room and down the stairs.

"I thought we did, too," he hollered. "I thought we were one and the same. It would seem not. I thought you wanted to live free?"

He ran to the banister, looking down to the first floor. Just as Winnie was walking out the front door, she could hear him yelling down at her, "Hypocrite!"

Twenty-One

One of Our Own

Once again, Winnie was alone and on the streets. Though, this time was much different. Now, she had money in her pocket. She could even be called a wealthy woman.

The other change was within her. She accepted a lifestyle although she was not living it. That all changed. She no longer would trust, care, or love. She would live her life fully for her own behalf.

She had to be sparing with her money, make it last till she came up with a way of making more money. Though she didn't want to, she rented a small one room, overlooking the harbor.

Whenever she left the apartment, she received propositions from men, on the streets, in the bars and restaurants, everywhere she went. It would be an easy answer to her predicament, except it was a road she dare not go down. She needed a plan, and soon, or eventually she would have no alternative.

It was late in the night, the taverns were closed, and the streets were empty and silent. A knock at the door woke Winnie with a start. Her mind raced about whom it might be. Even her landlord would not be at her door at such a late hour.

Dressed in her nightgown, she stepped up to the door, holding her gun before her.

"Who is it?" she called out.

"The police, ma'am, sorry to wake you, but there's been a crime just below. We'd like to ask you a few questions," a husky voice called back. From the term *we*, she suspected at least two officers.

"It won't take long, ma'am."

The moment she unlocked the door, it flew open, knocking the gun out of her hand, slamming her to the floor.

Instantly, two large dark men rushed into the room. Before, she could stir or make a sound; they lifted her to her feet. The first man held her from behind, as the second man brought his fist full speed across her chin, knocking her unconscious.

***

When she opened her eyes, again, the world was a blur. She could barely make out the three figures standing before her. Trying to move, she realized she was bound, hands and feet, and tied to a wooden frame.

As her sight cleared, she recognized two of the men as the ones who attacked her in her room. The third man was much smaller, in height and weight, an older distinguished looking gentleman. He stood in front of Winnie, eyeing her like a prized trophy.

"You've outdid yourselves this time, gentlemen. She is very lovely," he announced, turning from her, and then handing one of the men a large wad of money. "I won't need anything for at least a month."

"Thank you, sir," they said in unison, leaving the room.

It was then, Winnie realized they were in an attic. The walls, ceiling, floor, and the frame she was tied to were all made of old dry wood. Directly before her, on the far wall was a large floor-to-ceiling window. Looking out, she could see the sky and the tops of other buildings. They were in the center of New Orleans.

This strange little man moved in closer to her. His clothing was that of a gentleman, only that was as far as the word described him. The salt and pepper hair on his head was poorly kept, strands reaching out into space like a tree in the park on a winter's day. His mustache of the same color was thick and bushy. With a closer look, she could see breadcrumbs mixed into the weave of his hairs. He spoke directly into her face. His breath was foul as a chicken coop. Caused not only by the fragments of food stuck between his teeth, but the poor digestion he was experiencing, and of course, poor dental hygiene.

"We are going to have such fun, my dear," he whispered, his hands moving over her like a snake.

It was at that moment; Winnie realized that to be raped by this man would be the least of her worries. There was a madness about him that screamed for violence; only sadistic cruelty would bring him to the brink of the bliss he craved. A bliss brought on only by the shrieks of pain, pleads for mercy, and the taste of blood. His happiness was paramount to the wants and needs of others, as it should be when living by the philosophies she had adopted. The old ways need to be abandoned. She had to consider it all. She needed a plan and quick, or she would not survive.

"You paid a lot of money for me, Monsieur," she stated coldly.

"Don't you worry your pretty little head over such things. I'll get my money's worth."

"You've been wasting your money."

"I'll be the judge of that."

"No, I mean you don't need to pay thugs hundreds of dollars to get what you want. Pretty women are a penny a dozen. I could bring them to you for a fraction of what you're paying now."

"And how will you do that?" he asked.

"I have my ways."

He laughed, "Could it be we have found one of our own, you heartless wench. Tell me, why should I trust you?"

"Can you afford not to."

"If you cross me, you're a dead woman; you know that, don't you?"

"I understand. I won't let you down. I just want the money."

He laughed even harder, as he cut her loose.

****

Doctor Martin Furieux emigrated from France to New Orleans at a young age. Now, in his eighties, his medical practice was down to a small manageable amount of patients, most of them under his guidance for years. Although nearly fully retired, he never stopped his study and experiments on the human anatomy. His findings he had contributed over the years, and was well-known for.

He never married and had few friends, which was the way he liked it. Many preferred to be an acquaintance, it was safer. Few ever crossed him.

He was a true libertine, godless, narcissistic.

It was no secret; the doctor was infamous concerning his perverted sexuality. Though quite impotent, he found ways of staying sexually active, in ways most decent folk would not so much as talk about. It was also well known that these exploits were performed with prostitutes.

What was not known was that these ladies of the night were never hired, paid for, they were kidnapped. Not only that, every woman who became his captive never left the doctor's abode, alive that is. Winnie had no idea what dangers lay ahead, and how evil was the man she had now partnered with.

Twenty-Two

Life Is Not Fair

Life was looking up for Winnie. She'd moved into a fine two-room apartment in a better part of town, far from the harbor. It was a lonely life; there was no one she called friend, for she trusted no one. Her income from working for Doctor Martin Furieux was more than enough to live comfortably and still put a little aside.

Sad to say, Winnie had become scrupulously heartless. She had made her bed, and was willing to sleep in it. And for all outward appearances, she had made the better decision.

Once each week, at nightfall, Winnie would dress up and head down to the harbors. There was always a large variety of ladies of the evening walking along the harbor. Thankfully, Doctor Furieux was not a picky man.

Her scheme was to approach one of the women who was standing alone waiting for an offer.

"Are you working?" she'd ask.

"No, they pay me to hold up this building! Of course, I'm working, what ya think?" the woman would reply, sarcastically.

"I've got a client who likes having two women at a time. He's wealthy, the money's good."

"What do ya call good?"

"Ten. Sometimes more, if he's pleased."

That was all it took. An offer of ten was three times what she might expect from an entire night's work. A drive to the doctor's home in a cab always put the woman's mind at ease. Surely, this was her lucky night.

Doctor Furieux greeted them at the door. The three would gather in the parlor for drinks. The one served to the woman was laced with a sleeping potion, something easily accessible to a well-known physician as Doctor Furieux.

And then came the hard part, helping the doctor bring the women up to the attic, and tying her up within the wooden frame. Still, she couldn't complain, the money was good. Before the woman came to, Winnie was long gone.

Now this is where truth and fantasy collide. As heartless a Winnies' actions where, she only suspected the woman was raped many times over the next few days, it wasn't a nice thing to prey on the woman, nevertheless that was what Winnie believed.

As godless as Winnie supposed herself to be, she believed all she was doing was allowing the late night doctor to commit his sins for a price and then let them go home. She held conviction the women were losing little, and that being raped was just another way of life they were used to, trying their best to make a living. When all is said and done; ten dollars for an evening with an impotent old man was well worth it.

However, there was far more to it than that. Something Winnie never heard of, nor would she believe if she were told. Being impotent, Doctor Furieux created more dangerous games to play to bring him to the edge of bliss with these women. Things she or anyone else could never imagine. Much of it required the loss of blood, bringing the victim near to the point of death, only to rescue her, as to be used again the following day. This went on and on till all blood was drained from the victim. This was when Winnie was contacted that a new girl was needed.

Surely, these were women who knew the score; it was easy money for them, so she believed.

Only, in time Winnie questioned the feel of the hard wind behind it all, pressing against her. How long could it go on till Winnie understood the scheme and would no longer accept the cost, or would she?

****

Two weeks passed with no word from Doctor Furieux. This worried Winnie; she had become fully reliant on him, being her only source of income. Fearing the worst, she went to visit his home.

There was no answer to her knock on the door. It surprised her to find the door unlocked. Entering, she found none of the help available. This meant only one thing. The doctor was up in the attic, and wanted to be alone with his prey.

Winnie stood at the door of the attic and knocked.

"Go away! I told you I wanted to be alone!"

"It's me, sir; it's Winnie."

He hesitated before answering. "Come in," he finally called out.

The first thing she saw when entering was the single floor to ceiling window at the far wall, letting in the light, and its view of the city. She turned to see the captive woman bound in the wooden frame.

The woman was naked, unconscious, covered with cuts and soars. There was a large basin at her feet that caught her blood. Clearly, she was near death from lack of blood and nothing to eat for days. Her bones protruded, her ribcage like rows plowed in a field, her arms like sparrow's wings, her legs were sticks.

"My God, what have you done?" Winnie exclaimed in shock.

"I forbid you to use that name in my presence," he shouted back. "What does it look like I'm doing? My pleasure is my own business, and no one else's, especially not God's. I believed you were one of us, a libertine. Instead, I find you to be just another hypocrite." He moved in closer to the woman, cutting her free, and catching her before she fell to the floor.

He spoke as he dragged her to the window. "I feel benevolent today. What say we set her free; send her soul to her God."

With that, he tossed her through the window. Glass shards flew in every direction. The woman seemed suspended in the air for a moment. The next instant, she dropped like a stone.

"No!" Winnie cried out.

Doctor Furieux stood by the window, laughing.

A few minutes later, the police were at the door. They took Doctor Martin Furieux away. They brought Winnie in for questioning, and later released her.

****

If not the most upsetting thing we learn when we journey from childhood to adulthood is that *Life is not fair*. We see it all around, and most often there is nothing we can do about it. We can only shrug and move on.

Such was the case of Doctor Martin Furieux. Being a wealthy and renowned citizen of New Orleans, he was given special treatment from the outset.

His defense was simple. The dead woman was his assistant, helping him with experiments in his laboratory in the attic. Her fall through the window was an accident. The reason she was naked and her body covered with deep cuts was they were working on a new formula for a healing cream, an ointment for healing cuts and bruises.

Doctor Furieux claimed the experiment was a complete success. He promised to hand over the recipe, free of charge, to the Confederate military. For which he received an accommodation from President Jefferson Davis. As well, he was willing to pay all court cost. Doctor Martin Furieux was claimed innocent and sent home within the hour.

Chapter Twenty-Three

An Unseen Beast

At the doctor's request, Winnie accepted an invitation to talk business with him at his home.

Doctor Furieux burst into a fit of laughter. "You are such a hypocrite," he told Winnie. "I thought I found a like-minded libertine. Now, it seems you're just as weak and foolish as most other people."

"I just don't want to be a part of murder," Winnie argued.

"You are showing your ignorance, now. A true libertine lives by truth and fact, not feelings. If there was such a thing as sin, one sin would be no greater than the other. If there were such a thing as God, his very laws would prove he is man-made. The libertine knows there is only one god, and that is the self. He knows there is no such thing as sin, only going against his own true nature."

He poured them both a brandy, offering one to Winnie; she knew if she drank it, she would become one of his victims.

He continued, "Very well, your services are no longer needed. But there is one last job I'm offering you, if you want to make a good amount of money. And it has nothing to do with bringing girls here."

"What is that?" she asked.

"In a week's time, I am hosting a large gala, here. I've sent invites to the elite of the city. I'd like to have you attend. I will pay you handsomely, if you do."

"Why me...?"

"It's just good business to have as many beautiful women attending as possible."

Winnie thought this all very strange, as the doctor was never a socialite. Still, the thought of making a large amount of money just to attend a party was impossible to turn down. A price was settled on; Winnie agreed to attend.

****

Fortunately, Doctor Furieux, though well-known, was not well liked. Invitations to his party were extended to the Mayor and many other city officials. As well, many of the well-to-do of the city wanted nothing to do with him. This is not to say all invitations were turned down. Many of the city's wealthy accepted. These were mostly opportunists, gossips, and those looking for a night of feasting at the expense of someone else.

Though Doctor Furieux was disappointed as to who showed up, he was pleased with the amount of guests. It was more than enough to put his scheme into action.

When Winnie arrived, she still was unsure what her role was in the evening's play.

The entire first floor was crowded by no fewer than one hundred of New Orleans' upper crust. The dim of conversation was near deafening. Doctor Furieux hired extra help for the evening. There were tables of food and drink, which needed replenishing every hour.

Winnie found the doctor off in the corner of one of the rooms, alone, eyeing the goings-on with pleasure.

"I still don't understand why I'm here," Winnie said, standing beside him, watching the crowd.

"I just wanted to show my appreciation for all the work you've done for me. Now that you will no longer be working for me, think of it as a going away celebration. Have you had something to eat and drink?"

"Yes, I have."

"Make sure you have some of the champagne, before it's all gone."

"Thank you, I've had a glass."

"Good," he said, smiling. "I want you to enjoy yourself. I want you to be a part of this moment."

"What do you mean?" Winnie asked, sounding suspicious.

"You are about to witness the finale of an experiment that I have been working on for years, the greatest scientific achievement of our times."

"What are you saying?" Winnie asked, now alarmed.

"Since recorded history, mankind has searched for the perfect aphrodisiac, something that will sexually stimulate a human being. Think of it…pleasure beyond your imagination."

"You're mad," Winnie declared.

"Am I? You won't think so in the morning, for tonight all your dreams will come true, as it will for everyone here. If you drank a glass of Champagne, you've been dosed." He reached over to one of the tables, taking up a glass of Champagne. "Allow me to join you," he laughed. He swallowed it down in two quick gulps. "Now, we'll see who's mad."

An ocean of fear washed over Winnie. What was she to do? It was all too late. She moved about the room. She felt no change. Perhaps, the doctor was wrong, his potion wouldn't work. Then, she began to feel the effects.

It started with a strong feeling in her feet and legs, an almost effervescent sensation. Actually, it was all very pleasant. Looking about, it was obvious other guests were feeling the effects. They became louder, some of them laughing insanely, others crying hellishly. Just as the doctor predicted, some people began taking off their clothes. Then, it hit her fully.

It was like being swallowed whole by some unseen beast. She was completely consumed by the drug. Her eyesight became tunneled; all sounds were no more than echoes in the cave that was her mind. She couldn't move in the directions she wanted, having no control over her muscles or her thoughts. Nothing made any sense. Her mind became an insane asylum, as did the entire party. It was torture within her skull, an avalanche down to the pit of hell. The next few hours were a blur to Winnie, only to wake the next morning in a most unlikely place.

****

For weeks, the gala held by Doctor Martin Furieux was the talk of the town. The newspapers ran articles every day. For months it was still discussed around diner tables. In time it became one of the many legends of New Orleans. The truth of what really happened long forgotten.

The facts are as follows: Everyone who attended the gala had at least one glass of Champagne. The drug inebriated them all, causing sever hallucinations. Some folks were found naked, leagues from the gala, some even miles from the outskirts of town. Many were injured, broken arms and legs, and burns from walking into the fireplace. Three people died that night, one a suicide who'd cut her wrists. The amount of damage to health and property was immeasurable.

As for Doctor Furieux, justice had been cheated once more. Under the influence of the drug, the good doctor was under the delusion that he could fly. Making his way to the roof, he spread his wings, so he believed, and leaped to his death.

Twenty-Four

Morning Regret

Jordan Saint-Ford was in his fifties with a keen wit, intelligent, and very wealthy, a true libertine with a self-love that could only be described as idolatry. He was a handsome man, in his own way, tall and well-built. He spent his days and his money for nothing other than pleasure, his own, of course, not caring about others.

It alarmed Winnie to wake up in a large bed, in a fine room, next to this man. Her movements woke him. It was then she realized she was naked. She sat up, holding the sheets to cover her.

"What happened? Where am I? Who are you?"

He laughed at the bombardment of questions. "Who am I? You didn't seem to care who I was last night."

"Why, what happened?"

"We had a prayer meeting, just the two of us." He laughed all the harder. "What do you think happened?" He reached out, slowly moving the sheet away, exposing her. "There, now isn't that better?"

"I don't understand how I even got here."

"That's a little blurry, even for me. Now, let me think." He sat up. Winnie re-covered herself with the sheet. "If my memory serves me, last night there was a gala at the home of Doctor Furieux. I was invited because I was a close acquaintance of Furieux, not a friend, mind you, Furieux never hand any friends. I remember you were there, also. I suspect Furieux dosed all of us with some form of drug, for whatever insane reason."

"He believed he'd found a true aphrodisiac," Winnie implied.

"That sounds like him, the old fool," Saint-Ford continued. "I suppose it worked, at least for us it did," he laughed. "I've taken many a drug in my life, but whatever that was, it was one of the strongest. Now, I assume introductions are in order. My name is Jordon Saint-Ford. This is my home, and you are my guest. And you are...?"

"Winnie..." she answered.

"Winnie," he echoed. "How charming...and what is your connection with Doctor Furieux?"

"I used to work for him," Winnie admitted.

"You did," he exclaimed. "Knowing Furieux, it must have been to commit some crime or transgression against God and man." Again, he laughed.

Just then, the bedroom door opened. In walked a woman carrying a tray on which was a teapot and three teacups. She placed the tray on a side table near the window. She was a tall, beautiful young woman, with flawlessly smooth pink skin like the center of a carnation. Her hair was long strands of gold, touching her shoulders. What was most noticeable was that she was completely naked.

"Ah, coffee served in bed, what a luxury," Saint-Ford proclaimed. "You remember Iris from last night, don't you, my dear?"

Iris poured out three cups. She came to the bed carrying two full cups. She reached across the bed, handing Saint-Ford his coffee."

"Thank you, my dear."

Winnie took her cup.

"Good morning," Iris said, bending down to kiss Winnie, who turned her head, averting the woman's lips on hers.

"What do we have here...morning regret?" Saint-Ford said, smiling.

"Listen," Winnie remarked. "Thank you for getting me to someplace safe, last night, thank you for your hospitality, but I need to go, now. May I please have my clothes?"

This time, both Saint-Ford and Iris burst into laughter.

"You don't get it, do you?" he said. "This is your home, now. You're going nowhere. If you worked for Doctor Furieux, now you can work for me. Make it easy on yourself, and do what you're told."

Twenty-Five

All is Vanity

Winnie believed that once she made the decision to live life on her own terms, she declared the war within her mind won. Except, she was wrong, it was only the battle she'd won. There would be many other battles to come. Once again, the voice of good and evil, Jolene and Lucinda clashed in her mind. Only now, there was a third voice, her own, loud and clear. This voice did not have any statements to make, no options, only questions. And each question only led to more questions.

If there is no God, why do I see nothing but order in the world around me? Some say it is only Nature, but who or what is the thing we call Nature, and how did it come into being?

If I am god, why do I have no control over my life, anyone, or anything?

If there is no such thing as sin, why does shame reside in me? No matter how I try to ignore it, there is a feeling of regret after certain actions.

If life is nothing more than the seeking of pleasure and the avoidance of pain, then there is no meaning. What does anything matter, if you die and stop existing? All is vanity!

Is God just a way that we measure our sorrow, a bandage on a wound that never heals? When I pray, why is it only my voice that I hear? Am I simply talking to myself?

What about all the world's religions and holy books. There are miracles connected with each. Do their holy books differ, or just saying the same thing – I doubt it. They can't all be right! All can be wrong, but not all of them right.

Why is there evil in the world? And why, even though I chose to deny anything considered good or evil, sin or not, It still concerns me? It makes me understand I'm not truly convicted, and am indeed a hypocrite.

If God knows all things, why did he create a people he knew would sin? Why would he even put a tree in the Garden of Eden, and forbid them to eat? Knowing all along, they would give into the temptation and eat.

It was Adam and Eve who sinned, why must generation after generation suffer, paying for a sin they did not commit?

Who's to say there is only one god, why not many?

All the killing done in the name of God and at his commands, that can't be right?

But there I go again, not following the course I have chosen, a true hypocrite. I need to harden my heart, swallow my tears, turn from it all and follow my dreams.

Twenty-Six

One Particular Night

Mentally, Winnie had been in this place, once before. There was a strong likeness to when she worked for Madame Putain at Club de Messieurs. Only, the house was quiet and mostly empty with no lines of drunken men climbing and descending the stairs, entering her room, taking advantage of her for a price. Now, there was only one man she needed to please, and that was Jordan Saint-Ford.

Besides her and the beautiful blonde, Iris, there was Henrietta and Flora, both of equal beauty, Henrietta was blonde, and Flora was dark-haired. All were young white women. It made Winnie wonder if Saint-Ford believed her to be white.

One would think a comradery would form between the four women, that was not to be. Each kept to themselves, keeping communications to a bare minimum, which was just fine with Winnie. Sometimes it is best not to look in a mirror.

Jordan Saint-Ford was not a complicated man, yet his sexual appetites were intricate and thorny, and they were insatiable. He could be as demanding as three men, younger than he.

As with Club de Messieurs, Winnie continued her duties in a mindless state, as did the other women. You could see the lifelessness in all their eyes.

It would have been easy for Winnie to leave. There was no security, to mention. The problem was there was no place to go. After all, she was treated well, better than well, treated like a princess. Saint-Ford showered them with gifts, constantly. They received the best food, clothing and jewelry, as well as a cash salary each week, which Winnie hid in her room. As sad and miserable as she was, there seemed no alternative. So, she closed her eyes and mind, lowered her head and trudged forward.

Saint-Ford was a homebody, seldom leaving the house. Although, once each month, Saint-Ford would leave to play cards at one of his gentlemen friends' home. At first his excursion might be considered a day off, a holiday. Only, it turned bad by late in the night.

Saint- Ford would return with a few of his card-playing friends, all of them drunken old men, feeling randy. There was nothing else to do than obey, giving in to the whims of these inebriated buffoons. Thankfully, they were never as demanding as Saint-Ford. And if they were, they were too drunk to perform. They would fall asleep in minutes. Again, there was nothing to do other than trudge on until morning.

****

It was one particular night; one of Saint-Ford's gambling nights, different arrangements were made. The host of these weekly soirees lived in a fine townhouse in one of the city's better neighborhoods. Like Saint-Ford, he had his harem of women, which he sometimes shared with his guests.

There was an ongoing, but friendly, competition between Saint-Ford and this man as to whose women were the most lovely, seductive, and obliging. Determined to prove the better man, Saint-Ford arranged for his women to be brought to the gentleman's home, on the night of their card game. Late in the night, once the game was finished, Saint-Ford would have the chance to show that his women were superior. This would be degrading to all the women involved. Nevertheless, it was all part of the lifestyle they'd chosen, and none complained.

The entire day, Winnie and the other women dressed, primped, and prepared like matadors gearing up for the arena. All gowns were tried on, modeled, and put to a vote. Every hair was put into the proper place. Perfumes were selected with care. This went on into the night.

Just after midnight, the women were gathered in one carriage to be taken across town. It was a calm night with few people out on the streets. Because they seldom left the house of Saint-Ford, they looked up and down the streets, pointing, talking, laughing and giggling. Except for Winnie, she sat quietly, staring ahead, uninterested. Her life was like a giant buffet of the grandest, most expensive, gourmet foods, only, none of it had any seasoning, and all the taste was missing. Life no longer had flavor.

It was passed one in the morning, when they arrived.

"We're here!" Iris shouted, pointing to the townhouse, as the carriage halted. "It's nearly as grand as where we live."

One by one, they exited the carriage. As Winnie left the carriage, she looked up. She saw the townhouse, and her jaw dropped. She recognized the building at once.

It was the home of Graham Dorsey, the man she trusted, and who betrayed her. The man she had loved, and still loved.

The women stood before the building, looking up, laughing. Winnie was frantically thinking of a way to escape from the inevitable, and then fate stepped in.

A loud gun blast sounded, echoing through the streets. They all looked up to the top floor from where the explosion came from. The entire top floor was lit up, all the windows shining bright. The next moment, the glass in the center window burst outward. The shards fell quickly to the ground, followed by the limp body of a man.

They backed out of the way, immediately. The shards of glass at their feet, and then the body hit the ground. The impact shattered the man's head open like a melon, blood spurting into a puddle.

The women began screaming, without ceasing, in a panic. Except for Winnie, she was in shock, staring down at the dead man's face – it was Graham Dorsey.

Just then, Saint-Ford came rushing out of the house.

"All of you, back into the carriage!" he ordered as he made his way around the body and to the carriage.

None of them moved, turning to stone, screaming and crying. Winnie stood still, astonished and confused.

"Get in the carriage!" he hollered, grabbing each of them one at a time, pushing them into the carriage.

When he came to Winnie, she pulled away, trying to run off.

He slapped her, hard, tossing her into the carriage. He got in, ordering the driver to move on and take them back home.

As they pulled away, Winnie looked out the window of the carriage to see people leaving the house, running from the scene of the crime.

In the carriage, the women were still whimpering, shaking nervously.

"Stop it! Stop it!" Saint-Ford shouted hitting them full fisted.

In time, they calmed, sniffling and moaning.

At the house, they entered. Slowly, one by one, the women walked up the stairs to their rooms.

"Where the hell do you think you're going?" Saint-Ford, standing at the foot of the stairs, called up to them.

They stopped, turned, looking down at him, questioningly, with exhaustion etched on their faces.

"What do all of you think this is, a holiday? Flora, Winnie, I want both of you to go to my room and wait.

It would seem the excitement of being part of a murder aroused him beyond measure.

"I'd rather not. I'm not feeling well," Winnie announced, shyly.

Saint-Ford rushed up the stairs to confront her.

"Hold her!" he ordered.

The other women took hold of Winnie. They smiled with delight, as Saint-Ford punched Winnie in the stomach a half dozen times.

"Let her go," he ordered.

Winnie fell down onto her knees, holding her arms across her aching stomach.

Saint-Ford reached out, taking hold of Winnie's chin, raising her face to his.

"Now, get up to my room and wait."

It was a painful struggle, still Winnie made it to her feet, climbed the stairs and then entered Saint-Ford's bedroom.

Twenty-Seven

The Great Escape

Winnie could not say on what day she realized she could no longer live in the home of Saint-Ford. Conditions only worsened, each of the other women were a backstabber, everyone for themselves. Saint-Ford became more demanding. His sexual appetite leaned toward the new and the different, some of it from talk he'd heard, most of it dangerous. His experimenting with drugs, mixed with heavy drinking, was slowly driving him insane. It was clear, eventually someone was going to get hurt, or lose their life.

If she was going to run away she needed to prepare. She packed a bag of her favorite clothes, keeping it hid in her closet. She also hid any money she could get her hands on. As well, she made a mental note of all the expensive items in the house. There was no need to steal too soon, they would know it was missing and go searching for whom to blame. It would be best to take them just before running away.

It was a shame to see how wise in the world Winnie had become, able to recognize danger on the horizon, yet having no clue about losing her soul. How could she? How can you know you've lost something you never believed you had?

She figured it would take a month to get to the point she felt comfortable in her leaving, only one day an incident occurred that would make her escape eminent and essential, and immediate.

Winnie was called to Saint-Ford's bedroom, as she had so many times before. She prepared herself, before knocking on the door.

"Come in," Saint-Ford called out.

Entering, her eyes went to Saint-Ford standing before his canapé bed. He wore a tick, royal blue house robe. It was obvious he was naked underneath.

Next, what caught her eye was who was standing in the center of the room. It was a young girl, white, blonde, pretty in the face. She couldn't have been older than nine, though possibly a bit younger. Her sad blue eyes were red and swollen from crying. Her shoulder-length hair was knotted and encrusted. The dress she wore came to her knees; it was filthy to the point the color was indistinguishable, tattered and torn. She was barefoot, her feet cut and bleeding. It was obvious she was a street urchin, living on the boulevards of the city. Her body frail as a sparrow with her bones poking out of her thin skin. She was covered in soot from head to toe, and smeared across her face.

"Take this creature and clean her up!" Saint-Ford ordered.

"Yes, sir," Winnie replied, walking to the girl and taking her by the hand. "Come with me, child," she said softly. At the door, Winnie turned to Saint-Ford. "Her dress is pitiful. Once I get her cleaned up, what should I dress her in?"

"No need," he answered back, smiling. "Just bring her back clean. And by the way, you can join us. The more the merrier, I always say. This should be a very interesting afternoon," he laughed.

Winnie went into shock, nearly swooning. She had watched his sexual exploits become more despicable with each month, surpassing anything a decent person would call normal. However those acts were performed with other adults who could have said no and left, penniless true, still, they could decline.

This was more monstrous than anything Winnie could imagine. This was just a frightened child. Winnie had remained silent during many atrocities, only this was going too far, even for her. She had to say something.

"You don't mean...?" she asked, pointing to the girl.

"Of course, that's what I mean," he responded.

"But she's just a child!"

"That's the point; that's what makes it more exciting. Now, do what you're told, and hurry. I don't like waiting."

"I won't do it," Winnie said in defiance.

Saint-Ford marched up to her. In the next breath, he reached back, bringing his hand swiftly forward; he slapped her across her face, hard, knocking her to the floor. The little girl scurried across the room, hiding behind an armchair like a frightened mouse.

"Get up and do what I tell you!" Saint-Ford growled.

Getting to her feet, Winnie reached out, taking the girl by the hand. "Come with me, child. Everything's gonna be all right."

The girl cautiously took Winnie's hand. Slowly, they exited the room.

Winnie meant what she said. Somehow, everything was going to be all right. Somehow!

Winnie took the girl down to the kitchen, where the staff filled a tub with hot water in the center of the room.

"What is your name?" Winnie asked.

The girl looked blankly into space, taking little notice of Winnie.

"My name's Winnie, what's yours?"

Still no answer, yet she looked at Winnie squarely. Winnie smiled at her. This put her at ease. She halfheartedly smiled back.

Winnie pointed to the tub of water. "You need to take a bath. Would you like me to help take off your clothes?"

The girl quickly took off her dress and plunged into the tub.

Winnie got on her knees, taking a washcloth and soap to the child.

"I gotta dress she can have. It don't fit me no more. It'll be too big for her, but at least it's somethin'," said one of the women working in the kitchen.

"That'll be fine," Winnie said.

When they finished, the girl stood clean, wearing a dress twice the size of her old one. The hem was so long, she tripped on it when she walked. They took a scissor to the hem, to make it functional.

Winnie took the girl by the hand, rushed up the stairs with her, entering her room. There, Winnie rushed about for their great escape.

"Don't worry, darlin', we're getting out of here to someplace safe," Winnie assured her.

The girl was becoming more attentive to Winnie.

Winnie reached under the bed, fetching a black leather bag she prepared for this day, so long ago. Taking one of the drawers out of the dresser, she reached in the back, taking out the wad of cash she had saved. She went down the mental list of all the items worth stealing in the house. She dismissed the idea. With Saint-Ford in the house, there would be no way she could collect and not get caught. It was best to leave, while the leaving was good.

Hand in hand, Winnie and the girl tiptoed downstairs. Just as they approached the front door, as Winnie was reaching for the doorknob, as if out of nowhere, a hand grabbed her by the wrist. It was Saint-Ford.

"Where the hell do you think you're going?" he snarled.

Looking at the child and the valise, he immediately understood what was going on.

"Why you...!" he shouted, giving Winnie the back of his hand. The force of the blow threw her into the parlor. She fell to the floor, the valise flying across the room.

Saint-Ford rushed to her. He began kicking her so hard and fast, she was unable to protect herself. Each kick into her sides knocked the wind out of her. She couldn't breath. She was defenseless.

The girl stood in the doorway of the parlor, shrilly screaming. This annoyed Saint-Ford. He moved to her, slapping the child as hard as you would an adult. She fell to the floor.

The distraction gave Winnie time to catch her breath and gather her wits. On all fours, she scrambled across the room to fetch the valise.

When she took hold of the bag, Saint-Ford returned to kicking her. She struggled to open the valise. Each kick made it harder to move, once again losing her breath.

Finally, she got hold of what she was looking for, pulling the revolver out of the bag.

In that moment, Saint-Ford stopped kicking her. Their eyes met, each knowing the next second would change both their lives forever.

Pulling the trigger, she got off one round that sliced into his throat. He brought his hand up to the wound. Blood poured out of him like a leaky bucket. He began swirling around the room, blood spraying everywhere. He tried to scream, only, a gurgling huff sound came from him.

Finally, he spun around one last time, falling to the floor with a thud, lying motionless.

Winnie struggled to her feet, holding the gun in one hand, the valise in the other. She looked at the girl. She was clearly shaken up, nevertheless she followed close alongside, holding on to Winnie's skirt.

In the hallway, the entire household gathered to see what all the noise was about. The kitchen staff stood off to the side of the front door, at the top of the stairs was Iris and the other women.

Winnie went for the doorknob.

"Stop her!" Iris shouted at the kitchen staff, standing near Winnie. No one would dare approach an angry and desperate woman holding a gun.

Winnie turned, firing two shots in the direction of the women at the top of the stairs. All of them ran to their rooms to hide.

Winnie turned to look at the kitchen staff. All she saw was sympathy in their eyes.

"Go...go, now," said the woman who had donated the dress.

Winnie opened the valise, placing the pistol back in.

"Thank you," she told the staff as she opened the front door, grabbing the girl by the hand. They flew out, slamming the door behind them.

Outside, Winnie knew she only had a few minutes to spare. She began running, pulling the child with her.

When they were well out of the neighborhood, blocks away, Winnie stopped so they could catch their breaths. It was then she noticed the girl was whimpering, crying like a fountain.

She put her arms around the child. "Don't cry...don't cry...everything is gonna be all right...I promise."

Taking a closer look at the girl's face, Winnie realized it was covered with blood – Saint-Ford's blood.

Winnie took the hem of her own dress, licked it to moisten it, using it to clean the blood off the child's face. That was when Winnie realized that she too was splattered with blood.

They needed to get off the streets, as soon as possible.

Chapter Twenty-Eight

Lost Love

Winnie desperately looked about, wondering what direction to turn. Then she saw it. On the opposite side of the street was the townhouse of Graham Dorsey. There was no way to think of this as an alternative, still, she was drawn to it.

There remained the faded bloodstains on the walkway and front steps where Graham died. She and the girl purposely walked around it.

Winnie tried the front door. To her surprise, it opened. They entered slowly into the dark hallway.

"Who are you, and what do you want?" a voice called out from the darkness.

It startled Winnie, she was unable to answer or back away.

The person who spoke stepped into what little light made its way through the slightly ajar door.

It was a beautiful young black woman, dressed in an expensive gown that looked the worse for wear, torn and wrinkled. Her hair was unkempt. She too looked worn, obviously from lack of food and sleep. Looking into her eyes, you could tell she had been crying.

"What do you want?" she insisted.

"I was a friend of Graham Dorsey," Winnie said.

"Of course, you were," the woman responded. "Everyone was friends with Graham."

She moved in closer to Winnie, staring into her eyes.

"You weren't just friends with Graham," she said. "I can tell. Graham had a way with women. I can tell by your eyes, you loved him. I understand. I loved him, too." The woman burst into a fit of crying, falling into Winnie's arms.

****

They sat at the kitchen table, eating what scraps of food were left.

"My name is Rosiline, I live here. Graham didn't have any will or relatives, so the city has claimed the building. They've already taken most the furniture. That's why it's so cold and empty. They will be back for the rest, and in time they will sell the building.

When that happens, I don't know where I'll go. That's why I've remained here. I don't know where to go."

"My name's Winnie. I used to live here, too. I left when I had a falling-out with Graham."

"Not many women were able to do that," Rosiline responded.

Winnie continued, "I was here the night Graham died. We were just entering the building when he fell dead from the window."

"Fell dead? He was long dead before he hit the ground from a gunshot. That means you must be one of Saint-Ford's women."

"I was, but I left."

"Why, is it because you killed him?" Rosiline declared, pointing to the bloodstains on Winnie's dress. "There's not much. The other girls took everything they could get their hands on, but there's still a dress or two upstairs. You're welcome to anything you can find." Rosiline smiled at the child. "Is this your little girl?"

"She is now," Winnie declared as she brushed the child's hair from her face. The girl was busy woofing down the small stale breadcrumbs.

"I don't mean to pry," Rosiline said. "But I knew Graham to only like black women."

"That's true," Winnie said with pride.

"My...you are *High-Yellow*."

The girl was just finishing the last of the crumbs.

"So what's her name?" Rosiline asked.

"Don't rightly know, she won't or can't talk."

"What's your name, child?" Rosiline asked the girl.

Still, the child remained silent.

"Well, you can't go through life being called *Hey You*. Let's think of a name. Something pretty, just like you."

The girl smiled up at Rosiline, clearly understanding.

"Let me think," Rosiline said. "I know. What about the name *Belle*? It means *beautiful*."

The child didn't answer, yet her smile grew wider and brighter, obviously pleased with the name.

Rosiline surveyed the now clean tabletop. "Sorry, that was all there is. That was the last of it. I don't know where we'll get food?"

"We'll find a way," Winnie said.

Rosiline stood up, walking to the kitchen door. "Some of the beds have been taken away, already. There are still some rooms that have beds. You're welcome to any one of them." A solemn look came over her face. "I was Graham's women," she stated. "I was his women when he died, so I was his last women. His bedroom was the entire top floor. That's my bedroom. Everything else you can have, but the top floor is mine."

"I understand," Winnie replied.

Winnie and Belle remained seated, listening to Rosiline climb the stairs to the top floor. When they heard the door slam, Winnie rose from her chair.

"Well, Belle, what do you say we go look for a bedroom for you and me, and maybe some clothes."

On the second floor, they found only two bedrooms that still had beds. They checked all the closets. There were only a few old dresses left. They were all a perfect fit for Winnie; all were far too large for Belle.

They settled into one of the bedrooms. The sheets were clean. Winnie found a few candles and matches to light them. It was beginning to grow dark.

All the rooms had fireplaces, though there was no firewood to be found. Finally, Winnie smashed a chair into pieces, placing them in the bedroom fireplace. In no time, the flames were high; the room was warm and bright.

Winnie tucked Belle into bed.

"Everything is going to be just fine," she assured the child.

Unexpectedly, Belle pressed her palms together in prayer. She wanted to say her nighttime prayers. She looked to Winnie with sad eyes.

Winnie said the first thing that came to her.

"Now, I lay me down to sleep. I pray the Lord my soul to keep. If I should die..."

Instantly, a fearful look of horror appeared across Belle's face.

"No...no, honey. You're not going to die. I swear it. Everything's going to be fine. Now, close your eyes, and go to sleep."

Winnie began to stroke Belle's hair. In a few minutes, the child was fast asleep.

Winnie sat by the fire, staring into the flames, reflecting, wondering what would become of them.

She blew out the candles and got into bed next to Belle. The crackling of the fire lulling her to sleep, and then she heard it.

Coming from the floor above them was Rosiline crying. Not just crying, wailing in agony, sobbing for her lost love, Graham.

Twenty-Nine

To Keep Him Company

The next morning, Winnie and Belle woke early. Rosiline remained in the apartment on the top floor. All was quiet.

It took Winnie a long time to convince Belle that she had to leave and couldn't take her along. She needed to buy food and a new dress for the child, one that fit her, but mostly one that had no blood on it.

Winnie moved about the city as fast as she could, wanting to get back to Belle as soon as possible. She had plenty of money; however she was modest in her purchases, although, she spared no expense buying the sweetest little outfit for Belle.

On the way home, Winnie decided not to tell Rosiline that she had any money. Rosiline seemed a nice person, only trust must be earned.

Entering the house, Winnie found Rosiline seated in the kitchen, a half-filled bottle of rye and a full glass on the table before her.

"I got us enough food for a few days," Winnie said, placing the box of groceries on the table.

It didn't deter Rosiline from her quest to get drunk first thing in the morning.

Winnie lifted the dress out of the box. "I bought something for Belle to wear."

Again, Rosiline continued to show no interest in the world around her.

Winnie started out of the kitchen. "I'll be right down with Belle. How do you like your eggs?"

"I'm not hungry," Rosiline declared, taking up the bottle and the glass, walking around Winnie and then up the stairs to her lair on the top floor.

Belle was excited about her new dress; Winnie could see it in her eyes.

Winnie prepared them a hearty breakfast, after which they put away the groceries. Then they started up the stairs to their room. At the top of the stairs, they heard the front door open. Looking over the banister, they saw a group of workmen enter.

With Belle in tow, Winnie rushed to the top floor. Without knocking, Winnie entered the apartment.

Nothing was the way she remembered it, as memories often have a habit of doing. Everything was in shambles – unkempt. The window that Graham smashed through and fallen from to his death, no one had replaced the broken pane. The wind blew in, waving the curtains about like two flags. The breeze tore through the apartment, swirling pieces of paper about and causing small tornadoes of dust to spin about the room.

Rosiline was still in bed, sleeping it off.

"Rosiline...Rosiline, wake up! There are men downstairs. They've come to get the rest of the furniture."

Surprisingly, Rosiline jumped out of bed and onto her feet. She was fully clothed.

"Follow me," she said.

She walked to a book cove in the far wall. After making some adjustments, the shelving opened just like a door.

"Graham had this put in. It's a secret way back down to the street."

They entered; Rosiline closed the door behind them. It was slow going; as the stairwell was pitch black. They could feel their way with their hands and their feet on the steps.

At the bottom of the stairwell, Rosiline opened the exit onto the street. Stepping out into the light, Rosiline quickly closed the opening. They got away unnoticed, swiftly making their way down the street.

A few blocks away, they found a café, ordering tea all around. There was nothing to do other than wait.

"Now that all the furniture is taken away, the building will go up on the market," Rosiline said. "It won't be long before they sell it."

"Then what will you do?" Winnie asked.

"Oh, don't worry about me. I have plans."

****

Hours later, they returned to the house. Every piece of furniture was gone. Their footsteps echoed throughout, as they walked about.

Winnie thought that perhaps it would be best she and Belle move on with their lives, leave the building, and find a room somewhere. She had the money; only, she knew how quickly money burns away, especially when none is coming in. Though they would have to sleep on the floor, Winnie decides it was not the worst thing. There is no reason to go up to their bedroom because there is no bed.

Entering the parlor, Winnie removed a few bookshelves off the wall, throwing them in the fireplace, and proceeding to try to start a fire.

Rosiline started for the stairs.

"Where are you going?" Winnie asked. "I'll have a fire going in no time."

"I'm going up to my room, Graham's and my room," she spouted back, sounding still a bit drunk and slightly offended by the question.

Winnie said nothing, continuing to light the fire.

Hours later, night came; the house was dark, except for the parlor with the low flame in the fireplace. Belle sprawled out on the floor, asleep, using her folded arms for a pillow. Winnie stared into the fire, weighing their options.

The sound of sobbing echoed throughout the empty rooms. Clearly, it was Rosiline in the upstairs apartment. The sobbing became louder till she was wailing loud enough to wake Belle. Winnie decided to see to Rosiline. The weeping grew louder as she climbed the stairs. Standing at the apartment door, Winnie could hear her talking out loud.

"Graham...why did you leave?" she screamed.

Winnie opened the door, entering. She found Rosiline standing in the middle of the empty room. She staggered about, holding a nearly empty bottle of rye. Winnie had no idea where Rosiline had hid the bottle.

"Rosiline...you've had enough to drink, put down the bottle and come downstairs," Winnie said as gently as she could.

Rosiline spun around to look at Winnie, tossing the bottle across the room, the wind from the open window blowing hard into the apartment.

"For his soul is but a little while above our heads, staying with to keep him company! Either you or I or both must go with him!" Rosiline shouted, and turned, running forward, she leaped out the open window.

A second later, Winnie heard the thud of Rosiline hitting bottom. Winnie went weak in the knees, nearly falling to the floor. She regained herself; there was Belle to think about.

Downstairs, Winnie gently woke Belle.

"We have to go, darling," Winnie whispered.

It was true; although it was late, someone would soon notice a body sprawled in the gutter, authorities would be summoned.

Walking out the front door, Winnie placed her hand over Belle's eyes, guiding her around the body on the ground.

"Don't look, baby, don't look," Winnie said softly.

Rosiline was sprawled out on the walkway, the same spot her beloved Graham Dorsey had laid, not so long ago. Her blood pooled over the faded stain of his blood, mingling till it was impossible to tell where one started and the one ended.

Thirty

Desperate

It was a small, cheap room in a hotel in the dilapidated part of town. Winnie could have afforded better, only, now was a time to be frugal, especially with two mouths to feed. Everyday, Winnie bought fruits and vegetables, anything that didn't need to be cooked. It was lower cost than going to restaurants. Yet, even with pinching all her pennies, the purse was getting low. It was time to find a way to earn money.

Also, what was becoming a concern was Belle's health. Her appetite began to wane. Each day she ate less and less, despite anything Winnie said, be it pleading or demands. The child who'd been such a frail creature was now losing weight. Her new dress became too big for her. The sparkle in her eyes began to fade. Then matters became worst. What little food the child ate, she vomited up, later.

Fearing the worst, taking the last of her money, Winnie took the child to see a doctor.

"How old is she?" the doctor asked.

"I don't know," Winnie admitted.

"You don't know? Isn't she your daughter?"

"I found her on the streets. She has no one but me."

"I see," he responded as he continued his examination, double-checking his suspicions.

"Is it serious, doctor?" Winnie asked.

He seemingly ignored her, till he finished his examination.

"You can put her clothes back on."

"What is it, doctor?"

"I'm afraid it's cholera."

Winnie looked at him, questioning.

"It's an infection in the bowels. You get it from unsanitary conditions. She probably contracted it while she was living on the streets, as you said."

"Is it serious?"

"It can be. It's hard to say. She's a very weak and frail child."

"What can I do?"

"She needs bed rest. Make her drink as much water as she can hold, eat as much as her stomach will hold. I'd also suggest she be quarantined. It can be catching. How have you been feeling?"

"I feel just fine, doctor."

"That doesn't mean you don't have it. You might be infected. Sometimes symptoms stay dormant for the longest time. Even if you don't take ill, you may be a carrier."

****

Back at their room, Winnie put Belle to bed. The child did as she was told with no protest; she was so tired and worn.

Winnie sat at Belle's bedside for the next twenty-four hours. Mostly the child slept. Winnie made sure she drank water, whenever Belle woke. Only, she refused to eat. The one or two bites Winnie got her to eat; she vomited up, minutes later.

If she didn't make any money soon, they would be out on the streets. If so, Belle wouldn't have a chance. Early evening, Winnie dressed and readied for a night along the harbor. She didn't much like the idea, except it was all she knew. Besides, in just a few hours she could make enough money for her and Belle to remain in their room for two weeks.

Winnie looked back at Belle in bed fast asleep one last time before tiptoeing out of the room.

The harbor area was as she remembered it, cold, harsh, and dangerous.

Mentally, Winnie went to that place in the back of her mind where few thoughts came, especially fear and shame. She did what she felt she had to do.

Returning late, Winnie found Belle fast asleep, her breath shallow, her hair covered with sweat.

****

Sadly, over the next few days, Belle showed no sign of improvement, although, thankfully, she didn't seem to be getting any worse. Which was odd, as the doctor told her that someone with cholera either got better in time with rest, or died within a few hours.

Life became routine. Winnie spent her days sitting at Belle's bedside, and her nights walking along the harbor. Getting little rest, she too began to look and feel worn.

It was late one night, Winnie found herself in the usual situation, in bed with a stranger, in a shoddy little room, overlooking the harbor.

He was a seedy old man, an English sailor, by his accent. His body reeked of ale, rum, and tobacco. His thick white whiskers chafed her skin. She did her best to ignore it all, and trudge through it.

When he finished, Winnie got up from the bed, and proceeded to get dressed.

"Where ya think ye be goin'?" he said, sitting up in bed. "I ain't finished, yet."

"I know when a man's finished, and you're finished," She replied, making toward the door.

"Oh no, ya don't," he hollered, rushing across the room to the door. Fully naked, he stood before her. "Get back into bed, or give me my money back," he demanded, pushing her hard, sending her stumbling across the room.

He stepped forward. His clothes were slung across the iron bed frame. He reached into his pants pocket, pulling out a knife. Rushing toward her, he pinned her to the wall, the blade pressed against her throat.

"Listen," she whimpered. "I gave you want you wanted, now let me go."

He pushed the blade harder against the thin skin of her throat.

"Please…" she pleaded.

Finally, Winnie realized that no matter what she said he would not give in. She reached into her pocket, returning his money to him.

"Now, get back to bed," he ordered.

"I gave you your money back," she insisted.

He pushed the knife ever so slightly, just enough to pierce her skin. A thin trickle of blood ran down her throat, down onto her chest.

"All right…all right…stop, I'll do what you say," she gave in, making her way back to the bed.

She could sense him standing behind her. In her mind, she came up with a simple plan. She would reach behind her, hit his arm, deflect the knife, and then make a dash for the door.

It all happened so fast. She spun around slightly, hitting his arm with all her might. Instead of the knife moving away, it went deep into his gut. He let out a low moan, falling to the floor. He laid there, blood pouring out of him like a fountain.

At first, Winnie was shocked, motionless, staring at him bleeding. He reached down, pulling the blade out. This was clearly the wrong thing to do.

"Of all the stupid luck," he grunted as he pulled the knife slowly and painfully out of his gut.

When the knife was removed, the wound opened wider, the blood spurting out of him faster.

Winnie kicked the knife out of his hand. It went flying to the other side of the room. She reached down, taking the money from his hand. Before she could stand up, he grabbed hold of her wrist. She tried to pull away, only his anger strengthened him. He pulled her in closer, looking into her eyes.

"I'll see ye in hell," he growled.

With that he let loose of her, falling into unconsciousness.

Winnie backed away from him, slowly, never taking her eyes off him. She took hold of his pants at the foot of the bed. She took a large sum of money out of the pocket. Then she dashed to the door, rushing out of the room, down the stairs, and then out onto the street.

She ran down the block. Stopping, out of breath, she looked at the cash in her hand, before placing it in her pocket. The wad was soaked with blood, as was the front of her dress, her hands dripping red.

****

Back at the room, Winnie washed herself and changed her clothes. Belle was still asleep. With closer inspection, she realized Belle's breathing was shallow and irregular. She tried to wake the child, but to no avail.

"Wake up, baby, wake up," Winnie whispered, nearly in tears.

Winnie was beside herself, wondering what to do. She took Belle up in her arms, carrying her out of the room, out of the building and onto the street. People stared in awe as this woman carrying a child in her arms rushed down the avenue.

Belle was light in her arms, like a sack of feathers.

"You need to get that child out of here!" the doctor demanded. "She's infected! Besides, there's nothing I can do. It's too late. All you can do is take her home, make her comfortable, and help her to die in peace."

"There must be something you can do?" Winnie pleaded.

"Get it into your head. The child is dying, and nothing short of a miracle will save her."

In tears, she took Belle up into her arms, again.

"I'm sorry," the doctor added, moved by the sight. "Where are you taking her?"

"Somewhere…I don't know…to find a miracle."

Thirty-One

What child is this?

Again, Winnie was on the streets with the unconscious Belle in her arms. She was unaware of the stares she received from people. She had no idea where she was going; the doctor was of no use, going back to the room would be giving up, and death for Belle. There had to be an answer somewhere.

Turning the corner, Winnie looked up. At the end of the street was the Cathedral-Basilica of Saint Louis, King of France, better known to all as Saint Louis Cathedral.

Winnie had turned her back on God, and finally denied him. Still, if there was a God, surely he would take pity on a small child.

Winnie rushed to the Cathedral, up the flight of marble stairs, through the large wooden doors. The inside was huge with a high ceiling, everything, except the many wooden pews, was made of cream colored marble. Her every footstep echoed back to her.

There were few other people; with so much space she went unnoticed. Although, as she walked down the main aisle to the front, she felt like all the statues of the saints were watching her.

Standing before the main altar, Winnie fell to her knees, holding up Belle, as one presents an offering.

"I have denied you and your laws, living for myself. At times I have been your enemy. But, this child is innocent. Judge me, not her. If you must take someone, take me.

"They call you great, all knowing, and all-powerful. They say you are all loving and merciful. Then show it! Now is the time for you to prove yourself. Heal this child! I will do anything you ask. I will give up my evil ways, and live the rest of my life in your service. Only, please heal this child!"

Winnie stood up, walked up the stairs to the altar, placing Belle down on it.

She raised her eyes to heaven. This time she was shouting, her voice echoing throughout the building.

"Prove yourself! Prove me wrong! I've never seen a miracle. If ever there was a need for one, it is now!"

Winnie fell to her knees, crying.

As if from nowhere, a priest stepped up to the altar. He was young, a lanky man in a long black frock. He bent low to help Winnie to her feet. In her sorrow and confusion, Winnie had become deadweight. He was unable to move her.

"Why do you cry, my daughter?" he asked.

Looking up, Winnie nearly laughed at being addressed in such a manner by someone years younger than she.

Winnie rose to her feet, crying over Belle. The young priest stepped to the other side of the altar. He brushed Belle's hair from her forehead.

"Is this your daughter?" he asked.

Winnie made no attempt to answer.

He caressed Belle's face and neck, then bending low, placing his ear to her lips, and then pressing the side of his head on her chest.

Standing straight, he looked sorrowfully into Winnie's eyes.

"I'm sorry...but, this child has passed on."

Immediately, Winnie stopped crying. She took Belle's limp body up into her arms. Looking upward, she shouted, "I hate you! You had your chance. From this day forward, we shall be enemies! I hate you!"

The young priest was too taken aback to make a remark.

Winnie turned, holding Belle; she marched down the aisle toward the doors in the back.

Halfway down the aisle, she turned, shouting at the altar.

"There is no God!" her voice echoed, filling the building.

When she came to the large wooden doors, she heard the young priest call out to her.

"Can you be angry with someone who doesn't exist? How can you be enemies with no one?"

Thirty-Two

The Magus

They call it the house of God, open to all. On this earth, wherever there is good there is bad. The sacred and evil walk side by side, like legs of a table that hold it up, the other two legs being faith and disbelief. Remove one and it will all collapse.

There were few people in Saint Louis Cathedral to hear Winnie's rant. Most held no idea what it was all about. That is, except one figure standing in the back, listening, understanding every word.

He followed Winnie out of the church, and then down the street, carrying Belle in her arms. He kept his distance, not to let her know she was being followed. He stood across the street watching as Winnie brought the child's body to the nearest funeral parlor. The cost of the burial required every cent Winnie had left.

Returning to her room, exhausted, she fell on her bed. She could still smell the scent of Belle on the pillow.

There was a knock at the door – loud and hard.

"Go away," Winnie called out.

The pounding continued.

"I said to go away!"

A voice called out through the door, "It was your fault that little girl died."

This not only caught Winnie's attention, it angered her.

She rose from the bed, rushed to the door, and opened it.

Standing before her was a short, timid looking, little old man. He humbly stood in the hall, holding his hat before him. His white hair was cropped short. A bushy mustache, framed his kind friendly smile. His pale white skin was like graying snow. His eyes were large, watery, filled with sorrow and sympathy.

Winnie had all intention of cursing whoever dared to say such things to her. Only, when she laid eyes on this timid creature, she sensed a calmness take hold of her.

"Why would you say such a horrible thing?" she asked in a kindly manner.

"My name is Péché...Simon Péché. May I come in?"

Winnie backed away from the door; the old man entered.

"What is your name, my dear?"

"My name is Winnie."

"And what was the name of the child?"

"Her name was Belle."

He reached out, taking hold of her hand.

"I'm so sorry for your loss."

Winnie slowly and gently pulled her hand from his hold. She had enough of polite chatter.

"What did you mean Belle's death was my fault?"

"Don't misunderstand, when I said it was your fault, I didn't mean you purposely killed her. What I meant was your choices were the wrong ones. I imagine you took the child to a doctor?"

Winnie just nodded.

"And I suspect the doctors couldn't do anything for her?"

Again, Winnie nodded.

"You were at your wit's end. You needed a miracle, so you took her to a church. I understand. If I didn't know better, I would have done the same. You went to a God you figured was all-powerful, all knowing, and merciful."

"I don't believe in God," Winnie spouted.

"I can appreciate that," replied Péché. "But he does exist. He's as real as you or me. That's what I'm trying to tell you. You needed a miracle, but you went to the wrong source. He exists, but he has no power. The power was within you, all along. You just don't know how to get to it."

"And how does one do that?" she asked.

"By going to the true creator, he is all-powerful; he wants you to be happy. He will give you the power to make all your dreams come true."

"So, who is this true creator?"

"Come with me; I'll show you."

For a moment, Winnie was willing to take him up on his offer. However, her mistrust of the world forced her to decline.

"I'm not going with you anywhere," she stated firmly.

He smiled, slowly backing away. "I understand. You don't know me from Adam. I don't blame you." He reached into his coat pocket, he handed her his card. "Here, this is the address of my home. Come to me when you're ready."

He smiled, as he backed into the hall, and then walked away.

Winnie closed the door. She looked at the card in her hand.

Michael Edwin Q.

Simon Péché
Magus
1500 Lake Shore-Lake Vista

Thirty-Three

Return to the Streets

Rent was due, and her belly was empty. Winnie would be the first to admit she had no skills for making a living, save for walking the streets. Nevertheless, she dreaded returning to the streets. Not for reasons of morality, mind you. Firstly, it was a dangerous lifestyle. Every morning, the dead bodies of *Ladies of the Night* were found in alleyways and hallways. Many that survived the night were bruised and beaten. If a man refused to pay, there was not much a woman could do. She couldn't go to the police and make a complaint. It was a dangerous business, as Winnie knew from firsthand experience.

Another reason she was not too keen on the idea of returning to the lifestyle was that it was degrading. Men will treat a dog better than a *Streetwalker*. In time, none of these women escape depression. Many of them chose to commit suicide than continue on.

There had to be another way of making a living and Winnie was determined to find it.

For the next few days, Winnie applied for work all about town. All laborers' jobs, as she knew that was all she had the ability to do. She wore her shoes down, walking in every direction, bruising her knuckles from knocking on doors.

When applying, she remained to the truth. She could easily have lied, only, she knew that would come back to haunt her when she was found out, which it surely would have. It was best to tell them she had no experience, yet was willing to learn, work hard, and for less pay.

Without experience or references, no household would consider Winnie for a domestic position.

"*How do you get experience, if no one will hire you?*" she thought, and rightfully so.

It was the same with the shops. There was the bakery, the cloth shop, restaurants, café's, and taverns. No one was hiring.

Although she dreaded it, she visited the factories. Only to learn the factories used nothing other than slave labor, refusing to pay a day's wages.

It all seemed so sad and hopeless, as if life itself was working against her, demanding she return to the streets.

Finally, in desperation, she decided, like it or not, it was time to walk the harbor late at night.

The next few nights were a sea of faces and filthy rooms. They all told her she was beautiful, their whiskey breaths huffing and puffing in her face, their dirty hands on her, leaving their mark, soiling her clothes.

Again, Winnie shut her mind down and trudged through the nights. Luckily, she got through it all without any incident.

Within a week, she accumulated enough to pay her rent and pocket enough to buy food for another month.

She took a few days off, knowing it was a foolish thing to do. Once you step into the lifestyle, you have to keep at it, always moving forward like a shark swimming the sea in constant feeding. Money is magical, not only in what it can do, but in how in the blink of an eye it can disappear.

Winnie swore that no matter what, she would not shed a tear. However, the memory of Belle hung heavily on her like a milestone around her neck, pulling her down into the depths of depression. The visions of her past life mingled with the present. She had been nowhere, and was still going nowhere. All she could do was cry.

Among all those visions, one floated to the surface. She remembered the little old man who assured her of a new powerful life, one where all her dreams would come true. At the time, she only considered him a silly old man. Only, now she was willing to take a chance on anything, no matter how little promise it held.

Finding the card he gave her, putting it in her pocket, she left her room and was on the streets, again.

Thirty-Four

Go in peace

The *Lake Shore-Lake Vista* part of New Orleans was clearly the most affluent. There were no closely knit neighborhoods or shops, taverns, and townhouses. This was streets of mansions surrounded by well-kempt lawns and gardens, protected by high walls and fences.

1500 Lake Shore-Lake Vista was one of the largest and most spectacular looking mansions. Surprisingly, the main gate was not locked or guarded.

Walking through the garden to the front door, Winnie was overtaken by the perfume of flowers, and of all things, the scent of herbs, some of which she'd never seen before.

At the front door, she pulled the bell. A moment later, the door opened. She was greeted by a young black man in his twenties, wearing a dark suit. He was formal in his speech and manor.

"Yes, may I help you?" he asked in monotone.

"I'm here to see…"

Before she could finish, he shot a question at her. "Are you expected?"

"Yes and no," Winnie replied. "He gave me his card," she said holding it up for him to see. "He told me I could come see him."

"One minute, please," he answered, closing the door, obviously, going to check with his master.

A minute later, the door opened, again.

"You may come in," the young man announced coldly.

Inside, Winnie was captivated by the luxury and grandeur that abound.

"Follow me," the young man said, leading her to the sitting room.

The old man rose from his seat, walking toward her, smiling.

"That will be all, Dechu, you may leave us," he told the young man who immediately left the room, closing the door behind him.

"If memory serves me well, you're Winnie, right?"

She only nodded her response.

"You must call me Simon. Please, sit down," he said as he sat down in a large armchair, pointing to an empty chair facing him. "I think I know why you are here. Let me know if I have this right. Would you like something to drink, my dear?" he asked, breaking away from the subject at hand.

Winnie shook her head.

Simon continued to analyze her. "I assume you're here because life has not gotten any better for you, since we last spoke. I would presume your life has never gone well. People have always told you to trust in God. But he has never delivered, has he? So, I understand why you would not believe in Him. That is not where power lies."

"It comes from within you," Winnie added.

"Yes and no," he said, smiling. "True, the power comes from within you, only, where does this power come from? No one is born with it. It has to be received, a payment, or gift, for services rendered. All your life, you've looked for this power in a God who is nearly powerless. You must go to the true one who has the power, the true redeemer, and the true creator, he who is worthy of your love. All your life you've been told lies. It is time to grow up and learn the truth."

Simon paused for a moment, making sure he had her full attention, to see if his arrows were hitting their mark.

"So…?" Winnie questioned. "Whom are you referring to?"

Still smiling, Simon answered, "Lucifer."

Winnie wasn't sure what to say or do. Her first instinct was to just get up and leave.

"I see that I've shocked you," he said. "I understand. Years of being fed the wrong information has poisoned your mind."

There was a small table next to him, on it was a book. He took it up, handing it to Winnie.

"Here…this will explain everything." He leaned over and whispered to her, "I could easily use my powers to turn your life around. But that's not the best way. Go back to your life. And when you've hit rock bottom, you'll be back. Now, go," he said gently, still smiling.

Winnie felt relieved that he was dismissing her. She rose, backed away from him, slowly, holding the book, never taking her eyes off him.

Outside the room, in the hallway, she was met by Dechu, the young black man.

"They meet here every Friday night, at seven. You will always be welcomed," he said as he held the front door for her.

Again, she backed slowly away till she was outside.

"Go in peace," he told her as he closed the door.

Thirty-Five

It is Your Time

Winnie kept away from the book, as if it were a snake. It stayed on her nightstand, unopened. It was the last thing she saw before going to sleep, and the first thing she saw when she woke. If she didn't know better, she'd swear it was calling out to her.

There was nothing left for her to do other than return to the street life, each night walking along the harbor. In time, she understood why so many *Ladies of the night* committed suicide.

It was an unbearable lonely life. In a world where no one can be trusted, you dare not make any friends. The money was just enough to survive, never getting ahead. Feeling low in one's self, sleep becomes your only refuge.

After one particular, long difficult night, Winnie returned to her room in the early morning. The sky was gray with the glow of a sun still under the horizon. Winnie was so exhausted she collapsed onto her bed, fully clothed. Again, the last image she saw before falling asleep was the book on the nightstand.

The Hindus say there are three levels of consciousness: The *Wakened State*, where we live our lives, the *Dream State*, where the mind reflects the Waken State, and finally the *Thoughtless State,* where the mind finds rest and connection with the infinite. To some, all states are an illusion.

It was one of those dreams, feeling so real that you don't question it; seemingly a continuation of your woke life. Winnie found herself in a world of light and nothingness. From afar, she saw a black speck coming toward her, growing larger with each passing moment.

As it came closer, she realized it was a person walking toward her, although, unable to tell if it was a man or a woman.

With each step closer, it became clear it was a woman. No, it was a young girl. It was Belle.

She walked up to Winnie, stopping, standing a few feet from her. Interestingly, the sweet child, though dead, did not frighten Winnie.

They stood staring at each other for a moment, and then Belle spoke.

"Winnie, I've traveled a great distance to speak with you."

Strangely enough, Winnie was less taken aback that the apparition of a dead child stood before her and more so that she could speak.

"You can talk…!" Winnie exclaimed.

"I can on this side," Belle said, smiling. "First, I want to thank you for all the kindness you showed. And to let you know my passing was not your fault. I know you've blamed yourself."

The weight Winnie carried for so long was now lifted.

As if by magic, Belle was holding something before her, offering it to Winnie. As she lifted it closer, Winnie realized it was the book, the book Simon lent her.

Belle continued, speaking softly, "You have suffered for so long. It is your time, a time for your path in life to change, for all good things to come to you. There will be no more tears in your life. Read the book, Winnie. Open your mind. Trust in Simon. Trust in yourself."

Belle handed the book to Winnie.

Slowly Belle backed away. Then she turned and began walking the way she came, into the nonexistent horizon. Before she was out of ear shout, she turned, smiling.

"I love you, Winnie."

She moved forward, in the next moment she was gone.

Winnie stood there holding the book, crying.

The next instant, she woke. She was in her own room, in her own bed. Winnie was still crying. The book was no longer on the nightstand. She was holding it tightly in her arms, close to her heart.

Thirty-Six

Out of Love

The Light of the World
By
Demone Amoureux

In the beginning, many forces gathered to create the universe. Two of the strongest of these forces were named Qanna and the other was Lucifer.

They created the heavens and the earth. Lucifer created life, according to his name, which means light giver.

They separated the land from the waters, and filled the seas with life and the land with animals of every kind.

This grand effort of design weakened all the forces, except for Qanna and Lucifer.

The creation of the human race was left to Qanna and Lucifer. They did this equally, and saw that it was good.

In time, envy grew in the heart and mind of Qanna, according to his name, which means jealousy.

From that day on Qanna vowed to be the enemy of Lucifer, fighting against him at every turn, and since then there has been strife in the world.

At every turn, Qanna did everything in his power to hurt Lucifer, who remained benevolent, never retaliating.

When Qanna realized he was not powerful enough to hurt Lucifer, he devised a new and different plan consisting of two parts.

First, he would lie and slander Lucifer's good name. Fabricating stories that would sway the human race to not only misunderstand Lucifer, but to mistrust, and even fear him.

The next and second part of his plan was to lift himself up among the people. Until they believed he was the sole creator, the giver of light and mercy and all things good.

Finally, after generations of half-truths and misinformation, many of the human race worshipped Qanna as a god. Many people hating Lucifer, and fearing so much as mentioning his name. Till the day came few worshipped him, and those that did, concealed it out of dread of retaliation.

For this reason, I have been inspired to bring thee the truth, for thy sake, and the sake of the whole world. To write down the truth, proclaiming the glory of the true giver of light with all my might until my last breath on my dying day.

I say this out of love and a full heart. All your life has been a lie. You struggle through life confused, desperate, unfulfilled, and wondering why there seems no order in the world. I weep for you as you stumble about in the darkness, unsure and lost, hoping for an answer.

You are not hopeless or helpless. Take a new direction; worship the true giver of light. The power is in him who is all-knowing and all-giving. The one you worship now does not give but takes away.

Lucifer only gives. Once this power is within you, only then you may live your life as you please. With this power you will be your own savior, for you will be like gods.

Thirty-Seven

No Alternative

Winnie didn't know what to make of the book. In someway, she felt interested to pursue it, yet still she held an equally strong repulsion to it. For the time, it was best not to think of it at all for there were other problems on the horizon.

There was a cholera breakout in the city, mostly confined to the harbor area. Whole areas were isolated, hundreds of people quarantined, and dozens of them died.

"I feel just fine, doctor," she remembers saying.

The doctor replied, "That doesn't mean you don't have it. You might be infected. Sometimes symptoms stay dormant for the longest time. Even if you don't take ill, you may be a carrier."

Knowing the areas hit the worst, Winnie could not deny possibly playing a strong part in starting and spreading the epidemic.

Part of her was filled with shame and regret, wanting to stop her ways. However, if she were to live by her own philosophy, she must continue. After all, it was her life that mattered; her livelihood was on the line. What did she care if a few hundred died? It was just the way of the world, survival of the fittest.

Still, the sword of Damocles hung heavy over her head, night and day. The words of the doctor echoing, "Sometimes symptoms stay dormant for the longest time."

Would she be struck down with the decease? Why not? After all, it was just the way of the world, survival of the fittest.

That night walking down to the harbor, she was met with no resistance to enter the area. On the other hand, handbills explaining the danger were posted everywhere on the walls of buildings and lampposts.

Surprisingly, there were few people about. Looking through the windows of the taverns, she could see they were nearly empty.

Walking the streets, there was one sight she could not ignore. Every few feet, someone lay on the ground, in doorways and storefronts. As always, some were the usual past out drunks, although, it was clear to see many of them were ill, uncared for and unloved.

It was like coming on wounded animals, still alive, only caught in a trap, their sad eyes looking up to you, begging for mercy.

The smell of vomit and human waste hovered heavily in the air, as being two of the many symptoms of cholera.

Looking closer, she could tell that some of them were already dead, while others were only minutes away from meeting their maker.

The feeling of guilt, its weight would have crushed a person. So, Winnie ignored all thoughts of such things, disconnecting.

After walking the harbor for hours, Winnie realized she was wasting her time; there was no business to be had.

Turning, she headed away from the harbor. She nearly jumped out of her skin, when a hand came from nowhere, grabbing hold of her leg.

Looking down, Winnie saw a man's filthy hand clutching her ankle.

"Mercy," he called out in a voice so weak it was little more than a whimper.

It was too dark to see anymore than his shape, but not his features. In a fearful panic, Winnie kicked herself free, running away.

Back in her room, Winnie jumped into bed, like a child she covered her head with the sheets.

This was no life; this was a prison with no escape. She could think of no way out, nevertheless there must be one.

She uncovered her head, a shaft of light coming from the window landed on the book at her bedside.

She could think of no alternative. Fate was forcing her hand. In the morning, she would go to Simon.

Thirty-Eight

True-Life's Path

Winnie knocked on the front door, the book in her arms.

Dechu answered the door. "Come in," he said, smiling. It was the kind of smile that disturbed Winnie. A condescending smile that said: *I knew you couldn't resist, you have no willpower.*

Like the last time, Dechu guided Winnie to the sitting room; closing the door behind her once she entered.

The room was dark; it took a moment for her eyes to adjust. When they did, she caught sight of Simon sitting in a large chair, almost throne-like, smiling across the room at her.

"I've come to return your book," she said.

"Don't just stand there, come, sit down," he offered, waving his hand at a chair a few feet from him.

"Your book," she said, handing it to Simon, taking her seat.

"So, what did you think?" he asked.

"I'm not sure what I think," she responded.

Simon laughed. "Does the building have to fall on you? You're young, you're beautiful, and the world could be yours. Do you like the way your life has gone? Of course, you don't," he smirked. Without waiting for an answer, he spoke. "It's time for a change; you know it."

It was a struggle for Simon to rise from his seat. He stumbled across the room to a sideboard. With his back to her, she heard him fumbling with glasses, pouring each of them a drink.

"Napoleon Brandy…it's my only weakness," he said, handing her a glass, and then sitting back down.

"Well…salute!" he announced, holding his glass up in a toast, and then gulping his down in two swallows.

Winnie just sipped at hers.

"You're in luck," he said. "Today is Friday. We always have a gathering on Friday nights. Perhaps, if you meet others and see what we do, you'll feel more at ease."

"Why me...?" Winnie asked.

"Excuse me?" he replied.

"Why me...? I'm sure there are people who would jump at the offer."

Simon smiled. "I heard your rant in the church. You are not far from the truth. You just need some direction, but you must keep an open mind."

Just then, Dechu entered the room, unannounced. "Everything is made ready," he said, bowing slightly to Simon.

"Good!" Simon smiled approvingly. He turned to Winnie. "Are you ready, my dear, for a life changing adventure?" he said as he rose from his chair.

Winnie was unsure what to say or do. She stood up, blood flooding her head, passing out, falling deadweight into Dechu's arms.

****

Winnie woke, finding herself lying in a large bed, although she was not in a bedroom. The bed was in the center of a ballroom. She realized she was naked.

The strong drug was still on her. The world was a blurry haze. She was unable to tell if she was awake or if it was all a dream.

As hard as she tried, she could not clear her eyesight. Her mind swirled as if she were drunk.

Suddenly, she heard music, singing...a group of people singing. It was like no song she'd ever heard before. The song was a low rumbling drone, constant repetition in a language she didn't understand.

Getting out of the bed, she wrapped the sheet around her naked body. Standing on her feet was when she felt the full effect of the drug. This was not like being drunk.

She started toward the singing voices. A small group of about a dozen people were huddled in the corner of the ballroom. Their backs to her, all of them naked, men and women of all shapes, sizes, and ages.

"Show some respect!" growled an old woman, tearing the sheet away from Winnie. Now, she was as stark naked as they.

It was then Winnie noticed Simon was at the front of the crowd, leading them in the chant. She could see the back of his head. He raised his right hand high. In it he held a long sharp dagger.

The next instant, he brought the knife down in a jabbing motion. He raised the dagger up high, once more. It was covered in blood. It was a sacrifice. What or whom Simon had stabbed, Winnie could not see.

A shadowy outline of a large beast appeared before the crowd. It stood on two legs like a man with a wide muscle-bound chest, arms, and shoulders. Its red eyes glowed at them.

Inwardly, Winnie hoped it was the drug causing her to hallucinate, for nothing so nightmarish should be real.

Swiftly, the crowd turned on Winnie, rushing her. Hands grabbed her, pulling her back to the bed, tossing her down on it.

Many of the others jumped onto the bed. It was sexual pandemonium. Winnie had seen a thing or two in her time, still even she was shocked.

It wasn't only what she saw and heard that alarmed her. She was the center of attention. Between the power of the drug and the many people holding her down, she was unable to escape.

The bed began to spin, the voices echoed over and over in her head. It all became too much for her. She began to scream at the top of her lungs, only to be met with laughter. This was the last place mercy could be found.

****

The sun shone through the bedroom windows, waking her gently. Winnie had no idea how long she slept, only that she felt most of the drug was out of her system. Still, there was that morning after sickness flowing through her veins.

Sitting up in bed, she looked around. Elegance and luxury were the only words to describe the room.

The door opened, Dechu entered carrying a tray before him with her breakfast. Entering behind him was Simon, all smiles.

"Did you sleep well, my dear?" Simon asked, walking to her bedside.

Dechu delivered the food tray, placing it on her lap, and then he exited.

Winnie took hold of the tray, tossing it across the room. The clatter and shattering of glass caught Simon's attention, only it did not change his mood. He continued smiling.

"What the hell was that all about?" she screamed at the old man.

"That's not far from the truth," he replied. His response made no sense to Winnie. He continued, "You witnessed and took part in a Black Mass. You were blessed to meet face-to-face with the Dark Prince...Lucifer."

"That's not true!" Winnie shouted. "It was the drug!"

"You can believe that if it makes you feel better," Simon smiled. Reaching into his jacket pocket, he took out a large wade of cash, placing it next to her on the edge of the bed. "The congregation was very pleased with you. They took up a collection, passed the

131

hat, so to speak. There's two thousand dollars, not bad, aye? I would think by now you know which side your bread is buttered."

"I don't like it," Winnie pouted.

Simon's face went stern. "Stop being such a hypocrite, and follow your true-life's path."

Thirty-Nine

Penniless and Alone

Winnie remained in Simon's house for weeks. It was good fortune not to have to pay for rent and food. As well, Simon showered her with gifts, new clothes, jewelry, and perfume, never asking for anything in return. Thankfully, for some unknown reason, the Friday meetings in the ballroom weren't happening.

Winnie never left the house, spending her days in the library, and avoiding Simon and Dechu. Although, Simon insisted they eat supper together, after which he expected she meet him in the sitting room for lessons in chess.

It was late one Friday afternoon when there was a knock on Winnie's bedroom door. "Who is it?" she asked.

"Dechu...the master would like to see you down in the sitting room."

"Tell him that I'll be right there."

Fear took hold of Winnie. Remembering it was Friday, she assumed she was being summoned for one of the Friday night Black Masses.

"Come in, my dear, come in," Simon said in his usual singsong fashion. "Please, take a seat," he said pointing to a chair.

Sitting in the two chairs flanking Simon was a man and a woman, both old, yet not as old as Simon, both stocky and gray haired.

"I have someone I'd like to you met, my dear," Simon said, and then gesturing to the woman at his left.

The old woman stared blankly at Winnie, the wishy-washy flesh of her face like the color of biscuit dough sagging over the kitchen table.

"This is Madame Reine Tueuse. She is our high priestess," Simon explained. He then gesture to the man seated at his right. "And this is Monsieur Salete, one of the elders of our group."

Just then, the door to the sitting room opened. To Winnie's astonishment, in walked Madame Charbonneau, dressed to the hilt and looking as beautiful and elegant as ever.

"Wonderful to see you, again," Madame Charbonneau declared, taking a seat with the others. Winnie stared at her as if seeing a ghost. "You can close your mouth, now," Madame Charbonneau said, laughing, the others joined in. "Why do you look so surprised? You don't think I became so successful and rich on a whim? You're in the best place you could ever imagine to further your life."

Finally, Winnie sat down, looking from one face to another seated before her.

Madame Reine Tueuse took the initiative, "I couldn't agree more. We have a space for you in our little group, but the position must be earned."

Winnie continued staring, wondering where this was all going to lead.

Monsieur Salete took it from there. "The stars and planets will be aliened next week, the perfect time for a High Mass."

Winnie still looked confused.

He continued. "It is one of the most sacred times. We will all benefit, including you. What is needed is a sacrifice, as always. No need to concern yourself. We will take care of that. What else is needed is a Eucharist. That is where you come in. Fetch us one and you will prove yourself."

"I don't understand," Winnie said, looking from one to the other for an answer.

"Eucharist," Simon echoed. "It's the small wafer that many Christians proclaim to be the body of their Lord."

Winnie went wide-eyed with a look of dread.

"You don't believe such nonsense?" said Simon, as if questioning her sanity. "All you need do is to sneak into the Basilica of Saint Louis, where I first saw you. Go up to the main altar. There is a tabernacle on the altar; a small gold box where they keep a chalice, in it you will find the Eucharist. Steal the chalice and its content, and bring it back to us. It's very simple."

"What will you do with this Eucharist?" Winnie asked.

The entire group broke into laughter.

"You will find out, soon enough," Simon expressed amusement.

****

Dechu accompanied Winnie to the cathedral. Not to help her, mind you, she figured he was there to observe and confirm her theft to the others.

As they approached Saint Louis, Winnie felt her knees go weak. The last time she was there was when she carried Belle in her arms, hoping for a miracle.

It was early in the morning when they arrived, realizing their timing was bad. The cathedral was packed with parishioners; a priest was at the altar. They sat in the back, waiting.

In the middle of the service, the priest stopped, standing at the pulpit to give a sermon. It was then Winnie got a good look at him. It was the young priest who came to her at the foot of the altar the day Belle died. Recognizing him only flooded her mind and heart with more feelings and visions of that faithful day.

The young priest preached for nearly fifteen minutes. Winnie sat oblivious to what was being said, each word like seed thrown on rocky soil, unable to take root. Except for the last thing he spoke before returning to the ceremony.

For what shall it profit a man, if he gains the whole world, and lose his own soul

The words echoed in her mind, repeating over and over till they found root. Yet, his words gave her no solace, only uncomfortable confusion and fear.

When the service was over, the crowd poured out of the cathedral. A few minutes later, the only ones left were Winnie and Dechu.

"It's your move," he said, sitting back, watching as Winnie left her seat, starting up the aisle to the altar.

For some strange, unexplainable reason, her knees grew weaker with each step forward, her body shivered from cold chills as her head grew feverously hot.

Standing before the four stairs, Winnie stopped, looking down at the few feet of marble floor leading to the altar. That was where Belle died, before she placed her on the altar. Winnie stepped around the area, as if the body of the poor child was still there.

Winnie stood staring at the tabernacle on the altar. She opened its door, taking hold of the golden chalice, removing it from the tabernacle. Looking within, she saw at least a dozen Eucharist.

Her hands shook like a young tree in a storm, the Eucharist flying out of the chalice, and falling onto the altar. That was when a hot flash surged up her spine, exploding in her brain. First, went her hearing, the echoes of the cathedral disappeared, and then her sight went black. She stumbled backwards, falling, hitting her head on the marble stairs, out cold, lying in the exact spot Belle had died.

****

It was a tiny room with no decoration except for a crucifix hung on the far wall. She lay in a small bed. Seated at her bedside was the young priest, the one she met that day with Belle, the one who performed the Mass she attended.

"Don't try to get up," he warned, placing a cool towel on her hot forehead. "You're not well," he concluded.

"What happened?" she murmured.

"You're very ill. It's best you don't move. My name is Father Bon Coeur. What is your name, my daughter?"

"Winnie," she replied, again thinking it strange of a young man perhaps younger than she would call her 'my daughter'.

By the way he spoke to her; it was obvious he didn't recognize her.

"Do you have any family I can contact?"

"No, there's no one."

"I found you lying before the altar. What were you doing there?"

Winnie closed her eyes and sighed. It was best not to say a word. If she told him the truth, there was no telling what the consequences might be.

"I'll let you sleep," he whispered, rising from his chair and leaving the room.

Weakness covered her from head to toe; sleep came on her like a warm breeze.

****

The tiny room had no windows, making it impossible to tell if it was day or night. Winnie held no idea how long she slept. Opening her eyes, she saw the young priest sitting bedside holding a bowl and spoon.

"It's just clear broth, but it's warm, and it'll do you good," he said, holding a spoonful to her mouth. As she sipped at the broth, a thunderous voice called from outside in the hall.

"Father Bon Coeur, may I see you a moment."

Whoever the man was, it was clearly Father Bon Coeur's superior, and neither did he try to hid his disapproval

"Father Bon Coeur, what is that woman doing in your room? This is no place for a woman. I want her out of here, immediately."

"But, Monsignor, she is deathly ill," Father Bon Coeur protested.

"That is another reason I want her out of here. You do realize there's a cholera epidemic in the city, right now? I want her out this minute!"

"I'm sorry, Monsignor, I can't bring myself to do it."

"Are you going against my orders?"

"We can't just put her out on the streets. It wouldn't be Christian," Father Bon Coeur pleaded.

"Well, if you're not going to do it, I will."

Dressed in the same black cassock as the young priest, the elderly Monsignor rushed into the room like a storm of fire and brimstone. He took hold of Winnie, pulling her from off the bed and onto her feet. He dragged her out of the room, down the hall to the nearest door going to the outside world.

"Be gone, you worldly harlot," he proclaimed her as he tossed her out into the street.

Winnie bloodied her knees on the cobblestone. It took all her strength to get onto her feet and walk away.

****

The fever ran all through her, especially in her brain where it whirled like a hot tornado. As she walked the streets, folks avoided her, jumping out of her way. By this time, everyone knew the signs. They shouted at her, "Get off the streets. Call the authorities. Someone take her away." Small children at play laughed at her, throwing stones at her.

Be it luck or some inner instinct she was not aware she possessed; Winnie made her way back to Simon's house. She hesitated for a moment, standing at the front door, the sweat pouring from her. She knocked on the door.

For the longest time there was no response. She knocked harder. From the corner of her eye, she saw a curtain move.

Finally, the door opened. Dechu stood in the doorway. "What do you want?" he asked coldly.

"Tell Simon I'm here."

"He already knows. You're no longer wanted here. You failed to perform a simple request. Keep your illness to yourself and go."

He slammed the door in her face.

Determined, Winnie pounded on the door, once more, this time long and hard.

The door flew open. Without a word, Dechu raised his leg up high, kicking Winnie squarely in her gut. The force was so great, it pushed her down the stone stairs, falling to the ground, and rolling in pain.

It took a long time and great effort to return to her feet. She walked away slowly, her body aching and her pride hurt.

For hours, she paced up and down streets and alleyways. Every so often, she'd fall to her knees, and then struggle to her feet, again. No one helped, people moved away. They knew what was wrong with her. They'd seen it for weeks in the faces of the dead and the dying.

Her condition worsened. The body chills were unbearable, as the fever soared higher. Often, she would hold herself up against a wall, soiling herself and vomiting. These were the signs of the end.

The streets were empty. It was getting late. Folks were in their homes, calling it a day. The sun had not yet set. It was that time of day when day and night hung in the balance.

Winnie held no idea where she was. Not able to go on, to take one more step, she fell to her knees.

Perhaps, this is what I deserve, to die in the streets. Why not, after all I caused the epidemic. Others died because of me. It is only fitting that I die in the same manner. Only, what will happen to me. I have done nothing but live a sinful life, I know what I deserve. If there is no God, I will not lie in a grave with regrets. Yet, if there is a God, there is no hope left for me. Either way, I die, penniless and alone.

Though she had no food in her, she held a strong urge to vomit, perhaps for the last time. Surely, it would do her in. She raised her head and back, feeling the hot liquid rise in her throat. Bringing her head forward and down to relieve herself, she opened her mouth for the outpour.

Suddenly, she felt a strong arm, a man's arm, grab hold of the back of her head, supporting her. Then he took his other hand, cupping it under her mouth to catch the spittle, so it wouldn't land on her. Using a handkerchief, he wiped her mouth clean.

She tried to focus on his face, except he and the world were a blur.

He tilted her back, and took her up in his arms, carrying her away.

Is this the angel of death taking me to the afterlife? She asked herself.

Her head was against his chest. She heard and felt his deep voice. "There...there, you're going to get better. I promise you."

Forty

My Dear

Winnie was lost in her fever for what she could only assume were days. Every now and then, she achieved minimal consciousness. She realized she was in a bed, someone would feed her warm broth; move her about to prevent bedsores.

Often, she heard the deep voice of the man who saved her reminding her not to worry, his gentle hand caressing her brow.

In time, Winnie's health began to return. She spent more time awake than asleep, slowly becoming aware of her surroundings. She felt someone take her hand. She strained her eyes to see.

Seated at her bedside was a man, however not just any man. He was a young white man with the blackest of curly hair. His face was well-shaped, strong, yet somehow gentle. His eyes were emerald green with more than enough depth for a woman to get lost in. A row of white teeth gleamed, as he smiled at her. Winnie recognized his voice the moment she heard him speak.

"Are you feeling better?" he asked, tightening his grip on her hand.

"Am I dead?" Winnie asked, believing no man should look as he, only an angel could be so.

"No…not if I can help it," he laughed.

So many questions buzzed around inside her head. Only, the strain of even a short conversation was too much for her. She closed her eyes.

"There…there, you'll be just fine," he reassured her. "You just need more rest. Close your eyes and sleep."

Days later, Winnie's health improved; nevertheless, it was a long hard struggle. She'd fall in an out of consciousness, never able to as much as sit up, neither seeing nor hearing clearly.

It was all a mystery to her. Moreover, the strangest of all was the servant woman who feed her no less than twice each day. No matter how hard Winnie squinted, she was unable to see the woman clearly. There were hazy glimpses of her plump brown fingers and her round face smiling. Her voice was what mystified Winnie, it was so familiar, a voice from her past as familiar as her mother's, nearly as her own.

****

Winnie woke one morning, surprised how much better she felt. Not strong, not well, although clearly better. She even had the strength to sit up in bed. The bedroom door opened and in walked the handsome man, her savior.

"You're up," he said, smiling, walking to her bedside. "I hope you're feeling better?"

"Yes, thank you," she replied. "I don't want to sound ungrateful, but…?"

"I understand. You want to know where you are, who I am…everything. I don't blame you."

Winnie nodded.

"My name is Jonathan Gibbs, and this is my home."

"How did I get here?" Winnie asked.

"You were out cold, lying in the gutter. I couldn't leave you like that; so I brought you here."

Though she didn't press the point, Winnie was not satisfied with his answer. Here was a young man, so handsome that he surely had no trouble getting women. As a result, she was more afraid of him than if she were in the room with a hungry wild beast. Surely, there was an ulterior motive for his so-called acts of kindness. In her life, she had seen the depths of perversion some people revel in. She could only imagine that Jonathan Gibbs was one of the most evil. She thought it best to remain silent.

"Well, I'll leave you to rest," he said, slowly backing out of the room. "Don't worry about anything. The only thing you need to know and do is to get better. I'll check in with you, tomorrow. You see the sash next to the bed? If you need anything, just give it a pull. It's connected to the kitchen. Someone will come. Be well."

Smiling, he softly left, closing the door behind him. Winnie vowed that as soon as she felt most of her strength return, she would find a way to escape.

****

Late in the day, the bedroom door opened. Winnie sat up, stiffened, fearing it was Jonathan, again. Instead, it was one of the kitchen help with a tray of food for her supper. She was a large, friendly looking, black woman. Standing in the doorway, Winnie knew it was the woman who fed her over the last few days.

"You're lookin' better," said the women, walking to the bed, the tray before her.

As she approached, coming into focus, and hearing her voice, Winnie recognized her. Like being struck by lightning, Winnie knew the woman.

"Ma Cherie…?" Winnie questioned her own eyes.

"The one and only, in the flesh," she said.

"What are you doing here?" Winnie asked.

Ma Cherie placed the tray on Winnie's lap.

"Good to see you up and around. I have been feedin' ya like a baby, since ya got here. I guess ya can do it on your own, now."

"What are you doing here?" Winnie repeated.

"I run the kitchen," Ma Cherie replied.

"No, I mean how did you get here?"

"How do ya think?" Ma Cherie laughed. "A colored woman ain't got much say in where she's headin'. The South is like one big sea, and I'm in a little rowboat getting tossed and turned around. Ya get bought, ya get sold, and ya get bought, again. Master Gibbs is a good man. He's been the best so far."

"Tell me about him," Winnie asked.

"What's to tell? He's been rich all his life. His daddy was rich, and so be his granddaddy. Ain't got no family, anymore, lives all alone. He's some kind of bigwig here in the city, don't know exactly what. He got me in the kitchen, a maid for cleaning, and a butler, and he treats us all good. That's all I know and all I needs to know."

"...any women in his life?" Winnie asked.

"No, he stays alone, mostly."

"No, I mean Fancy Ladies."

"Ya askin' if he goes around pickin' sickly folk out of the gutter and bringin' them home to nurse, ya be the first and only."

A worried look came over Winnie.

"Don't look so feared," Ma Cherie laughed. "He ain't no monster. I've worked for monsters, and I know he ain't one. He's a God-fearing man. Still, I can't tell ya why you're here. It's befuddlin'." She turned to leave. "Eat hearty. I'll be back for the tray, later."

****

In time, Winnie was strong enough to get out of bed and walk about the room. Looking out the window, she knew the house was in an affluent part of town.

She turned when the door opened. It was Ma Cherie standing in the doorway, holding a bright, green, satin gown.

"I've drawn ya a bath. We'll straighten ya up and get ya into this...lovely, ain't it? The master wants ya to join him in the dining room for supper."

"I don't understand," Winnie pressed her. "Why me...?"

"Girl, I don't know. Ya gonna have to ask him. I do know one thing, though. If you keep stickin' your hand down the Gift Horse's mouth, eventually he's gonna bite it off."

A short time latter, her hair done up, wearing the green satin dress, Winnie stood before the full-length mirror in her room. Ma Cherie stood off to the side, admiring her.

"I'm beginning to understand why Master Jonathan brought you home," Ma Cherie said. Although it was meant to be a compliment, it worried Winnie. It did anything but put her at ease.

In the dining room, Jonathan rose from his chair to greet her. "It's so good to see you feeling better. You look lovely. Please, take a seat."

Sitting across from him, Winnie organized the many questions floating around in her mind. She was just about to speak when a woman from the kitchen came to serve them. Both Winnie and Jonathan went silent until they were served and the woman returned to the kitchen.

Before Winnie could speak, Jonathan took the initiative, "I'm sure you have a million questions."

Winnie suppressed the urge to smile. "I don't want to be misconstrued. I'm very grateful. I owe you so much. I owe you my life. But…"

Jonathan finished the thought, "But why are you here?"

Winnie nodded in agreement.

Jonathan slowly continued, thoughtfully. "I knew this would eventually come up. I've thought about it for a long time. What should I say? Finally, I decided the truth was the best way."

Winnie's interest was peaked. She listened carefully and thoughtfully.

"When I first saw you lying in the gutter, my heart went out to you. It made me stop and think. But as I looked closer, I realized you are the most beautiful woman I've ever seen. I couldn't walk away, so I brought you here, to have you nursed back to health. Now that I see you this night, I know I was right. You are the most beautiful woman I've ever laid eyes on."

Winnie was shocked. It took a moment for her to collect her thoughts. "I understand what you're saying, but I want to know what it is you want from me."

Now it was Jonathan's turn to be reflective. "I ask that you stay here as my guest. Not only till you are completely well, again, but longer. Stay a year. Let us get to know each other. You will want for nothing. If at the end of a year you don't want to stay, you can leave…no words said."

"So, you want me to be your mistress?"

"No, nothing like that!" he countered. "I will never touch you without your permission. Your room will be sacred. I will never enter it, uninvited. I just want some time for us to get to know each other."

It sounded all like a fairytale to Winnie, too good to be true. She would like to believe it, only never had she known a man of such honor who could keep such a promise. Only time would tell.

She had no other alterative, save for the streets. She held no money, and no prospects. His offer was all there was.

"Very well," she responded. "I'll stay for as long as you are true to your word."

Jonathan's face beamed with delight.

"Now, if you'll excuse me, I'm not very hungry. I'd like to go to my room."

"But of course, my dear," he said, rising from his chair in respect.

Winnie rose from her chair, walking out of the room. She stood in the doorway, looking back at him, coldly. "Oh…and I'm not *your dear.*"

Forty-One

Two Men

Time did what time does best, it passed on by. Though she was allowed to come and go as she pleased, Winnie seldom left the house. Each day, she spent time with Jonathan, as well as taking supper with him. As hard as she tried not to let him in, as they talked, getting to know each other better, she had to admit she was enjoying their time together. She learned much about him.

Jonathan Gibbs was born in New Orleans to a wealthy family. He was the youngest of two children. His sister, Dorothy, died when she was eight, and of all things, of cholera. His parents showered him with love, raising him to be kind and respectful to all. From the look of him, his dress and mannerisms, one could tell he was raised with a silver spoon in his mouth. However, inwardly, he never put on airs, and was liked by all, from slave to king.

His father was a well respected court judge in New Orleans. Jonathan could not remember a time he did not want to follow in his father's footsteps, nor could he think of any man he more wanted to emulate.

After years of applying himself to his studies, Jonathan passed the bar, accepting a position at the law offices of *Shafer and McCall*. In just eight years, Jonathan was one of the top lawyers in the city.

Sadly, it was at this time Jonathan lost both his parents, his mother that winter, followed by his father that spring. He was alone in the world.

Through his achievements, he worked his way up in the world to the position of court judge, just like his father. Though his father would have been proud, it was nothing compared with Jonathan's next accomplishment. In just two years as a court judge, the governor took notice of him, appointing him *City Judge*, in charge of and overseeing the rulings of all the city's *Municipal Courts*.

He became a man of great wealth, above and beyond his inheritance. However with great wealth comes great responsibility. He was alone in the world, acquaintances rather than friends, and room in his heart for a wife, yet there were no prospects. Not that there weren't any ladies interested in him. A man of wealth and status is always in demand. Still, not one caught Jonathan's interest. That is until he set eyes on Winnie. And the more he got to know her, his interest turned to deep caring and respect, which will, as we all know, turns to love.

****

What was no surprise was how the friendship between Winnie and Ma Cheri came to be. After all, it was only natural, a young woman with no family seeks out a mother figure and an older woman in a likewise situation looks to mother a younger woman. As well, they had similar backgrounds. Not to mention they enjoyed each other's company. The bond between them grew sturdy. That was why Ma Cheri felt comfortable to speak what was on her mind to Winnie who cherished the woman's wisdom and advice.

"Don't get me wrong, Winnie, you're a sweet beautiful girl, but sometimes I can't believe how foolish ya can be."

Winnie didn't get upset; she was never easily turned when it came to Ma Cheri. Still, she looked at her in confusion, waiting for the other shoe to drop.

"Wake up to reality, Winnie; ya don't even see what's right under your own nose. Ya got two men in your life that love and adore ya, to no end. They'd do anything for ya, and all ya do is ignore them."

"What are you talking about?" Winnie asked.

"Master Jonathan, for one, that boy's crazy for ya. He walks around all day pining for ya with his heart in his hand. He follows ya around like he was a sick puppy. He loves ya, and would do anything for ya. He's young, handsome and rich. and ya won't even so much as give him the time of day. I just don't understand you, girl."

"I'm not sure I can trust him," was Winnie's response.

"And whose fault is that? Certainly, not his, he'd bend over backwards to impress ya, and gain ya trust. You're the one who cut herself from the world, who put herself up on a pedestal, calling them self the higher power, like ya got all the answers. As for power, ya ain't got none. Livin' just for you ain't livin' at all. Ya may get hurt for tryin', but it's the only way. Take a chance. And I say, if ya gonna take a chance, ya best take it on Master Jonathan."

Winnie went thoughtful for a moment. If it had been anyone else besides Ma Cheri, she would have told her to mind her own business and walked away.

"Who is this other person you spoke about?" Winnie asked, not knowing who it could be.

Ma Cheri smiled, taking her time, making sure she had the young woman's attention. "Ya don't know, do ya? It's God, God almighty, that's who."

Now, Winnie was ready to walk away, only Ma Cheri was determined to have her say.

"Ya sit and listen till I have my say!" she demanded. "You're the one who turned her back on God, thinking ya the center of the universe. Well, where's it got ya? I'll tell ya, dying in the gutter, homeless with no friends, no family, no money, and no prospects. Does the world have to fall on ya, to know ya picked the wrong path?"

Winnie couldn't find a way to argue with that.

Ma Cherie continued, "If you're ya own god, ya doin' a poor job of it. He ain't never turned his back on ya, ya stupid girl."

Winnie's lower lip quivered. "What am I suppose to do?"

"Give them both a fair chance, that's what."

"How…?"

"Simple, start treatin' Master Jonathan like y'all want to be treated, that's all. As for the Lord, that's goin' to take some doin'. I'm goin' to start givin' ya Bible lessons."

"Bible lessons…?" Winnie echoed. "It ain't ever made any sense to me."

"That's because ya ain't got the spirit. I got the spirit. Don't worry, y'all get the spirit in time, I promise. Oh, and ask Master Jonathan to give ya leave every Sunday mornin'. We're goin' to church!"

Forty-Two

For the First Time

To Winnie's surprise, it was easy to return to her earlier ways, going to Bible studies with Ma Cheri and Sunday Church Services at the local Black church.

Far from being an expert, Ma Cheri knew her way through the Bible. She didn't have all the answers, yet she knew how to find them. And Winnie had questions, hundreds of them.

As for church, Winnie liked the music and the songs. Understandable, she did not warm up to the folks in the congregation. She was uneasy, finding it difficult that so many could be so friendly without a motive. After all, those gathering at Simon's home were there for their own benefit, and would do anything, including cutting one another's throats for their own gain.

It's important to note here that many of the congregation wondered why a black kitchen maid would bring her white mistress to a black church. Still, the question was never brought up in conversation, nor did it affect their acceptance of her.

In time, with the help of Ma Cheri and many others, the open wound within Winnie began to heal, and the gap between she and her creator was bridged. She was baptized on a Sunday afternoon, to the delight of Ma Cheri.

As for her relationship with Jonathan, that was a different story, a bridge too far to cross, perhaps? Jonathan was a man, and never in her life had a man treated her with anything other than disrespect, using her for their own ends.

Winnie was like a frightened sparrow around Jonathan, flying off at just the slightest sound or movement. Ma Cheri pleaded with her to give him a fair chance.

"Ya don't have to fall in love with him. No one can make you do that. Still, if ya close the door on him, ya may never know."

Through it all, Jonathan was patient, winning her over slowly, and biding his time.

Once Winnie opened her mind, as Ma Cheri said, her heart followed. At night, they would talk for hours. However, as much as she found him charming and witty, what attracted her to him the most was the way he interacted with people. Observing him from afar, she understood what a good man he was, what a gentle soul.

This entire time, Jonathan's approach was that of a gentleman, never physical, never as much as trying to hold her hand. Oddly enough, what once gave her comfort now annoyed her. She wanted so much for him to touch her and to touch him. Except, how could she convey this? She decided the only way was to tell him how she felt, and hope he felt the same.

It was after supper, and the two of them were in the sitting room, relaxing over brandies. Winnie sat alone on the divan; as always, Jonathan sat in a chair across from her.

"Jonathan, we need to talk," she said softly.

He giggled slightly. "I thought that's what we were doing."

"No really, we need to talk."

Jonathan went solemn. He knew what she meant.

"Jonathan, you know how grateful I am to you. You've been so good to me. No one has ever been good to me. Which is why I was so suspicious of you, at first, but now that I know you better, I know I was wrong. Please, forgive me."

"Winnie, there's nothing to forgive."

Winnie patted the empty space next to her on the divan. "Jonathan, please sit next to me."

When he was seated next to her, she took hold of his hand. He looked surprised for a moment, then he looked at their hands, and then up at her face, and smiled.

"I have two things to tell you," she whispered. "I don't know which one to tell you first. They are both key to what I want you to know. So, I'll just say them."

There was a moment of silence, as their eyes met.

"I love you," she announced gently.

"Winnie...!" he said, tightening his grip on her hand.

"No...let me finish, there's more."

A questioning look appeared on his face. Inwardly, Winnie searched for just the right words. Finally, she decided to come to the point, and blurt it out.

"I'm colored!"

He stared at her for what seemed like an overly long time, and then he burst into laughter. "What kind of joke is this?"

"I'm serious. I know my skin is light. I've been able to pass for white nearly all my life. But I'm colored! My mother, my father, my whole family is black."

"You're serious," he said as the laughter stopped and the smile left his face.

"I'm dead serious," she released her hand from his grip.

Jonathan spoke not a word, only staring at her. His silence spoke volumes, telling her it was over before it began.

"Don't worry," she said, "I understand the position this puts you in. I'd never hold it against you. I love you too much." She rose from the divan, and then walked toward the door. "I'll be gone in the morning. Thank you for everything."

Just as her hand touched the doorknob, his hand took hold of her. He spun her around, surrounding her in his strong arms. Pulling her in close, he pressed his lips hard against hers, kissing her.

The world revolved around them, her mind spinning even faster. When he pulled away, her knees went weak. She fell into him, her head flat against his chest, as she tried to catch her breath.

"Don't ever leave me," his voice hummed in her ear. "I love you. From now on, we will face everything, together."

She shook in his arms, crying so hard and long till his shirt was soaked.

****

When Jonathan popped the question, Winnie agreed to marry him on one condition and one condition only. She made him swear never to reveal to anyone her true heritage. This was not out of shame, rather out of caring. She understood what such information would do to his career. Jonathan would have proclaimed his love for her on the rooftops, only after a long discussion he agreed to her terms.

Jonathan suggested a small wedding at home with a Justice of the Peace. Winnie envisioned a church wedding. Already, the decision to hide Winnie's background would guide their life. They could not marry in the black church she had grown so fond of. The wedding would take place at the Basilica of Saint Louis, King of France. Again, this cathedral would play a part in her life.

It was so ironic to be standing in Saint Louis' in front of the altar, on the exact spot Belle died and where she fell ill, herself. Now, she and Jonathan stood there taking their marriage vows.

Strangely enough, the memory of it all, especially that of Belle did not disturb her. Although, saddened by the loss of the child, Winnie believed she was now in a better place, looking down from heaven with approval.

The wedding was a small affair with only a few business acquaintances of Jonathan's, and the house staff, which caused the turning of one or two heads.

Winnie's gown was cream, slightly off-white. She insisted on the color, not feeling right in an all-white gown. It took one of the top tailors in the city with his staff three days of fittings to get it just right. It was clear Jonathan would spare no expense to make Winnie happy. For the first time in her life, none of that mattered.

Adding to the dream quality of the day, Father Bon Coeur, the young priest whom she encountered before, and who nursed her when she was ill, performed the ceremony.

Everyone was invited to a small gathering at Jonathans home. Jonathan couldn't have been happier and more proud watching his bride move among the guests with charm and confidence. She dazzled them all.

When it was time to cut the cake, Winnie entered the kitchen for a knife.

"Can I help you, Madame?" asked one of the girls.

Winnie exploded into laughter.

Ma Cheri approached her, smiling. "Don't laugh, it's true. You are the Madame of the house, now."

Still laughing, Winnie announced to the kitchen staff, "Don't call me that, I'll always be Winnie."

"Of course, Mrs. Gibbs," Ma Cheri proclaimed.

The two women fell into each other's arms, laughing.

Everyone applauded the newlyweds, as they cut the cake. Neither Winnie nor Jonathan made a wish, as they made the first slice, together. Both of them had received their hearts desire, their dream come true, their prayers answered.

****

It went unspoken that they would not sleep with each other till they were married. Winnie was a nervous bride. At first she couldn't understand why. She'd been with so many men before Jonathan, though she hated to think about it. Then she realized that was the very reason she felt the way she did. All the times before were illicit, with no meaning, only a means to an end. Many had her body, however none every as much as touched her heart.

This was something different. An air of the sacred lingered over them. An act sanctioned by both God and man. She never had that before with anyone. Love was only something spoken about, although never proved true, something for songs and novels.

She wanted so much to please him, yet she did not want to imitate the past. Not with him, not with Jonathan. This was her love, her husband.

She gave of herself, her body and heart, so fully, she didn't know it was possible. Yet, the more she gave, the more she received. It was an endless cycle of giving and then receiving. Only to find you have more to give, and on and on it flowed forever.

As they made love, she cried.

150

In the morning, she found herself resting her head on his chest. She listened to his breathing, finding joy in every heartbeat. Watching him sleep, she found such joy she never knew possible.

Here was a man she would die for. Better yet, she would live for him.

Forty-Three

The Morning Paper

The Times-Picaninny
Mass Suicide
By Carlson Gannett

Authorities have long suspected a Satanic Cult harboring within the city limits. All fingers pointed to a Simon Peche of 1500 Lake Shore-Lake Vista. Monsieur Peche was a wealthy socialite, known about town. He was not only believed to be the leader of said cult, but it was understood his home was the meeting hall for their gatherings.

Monsieur Peche was put under surveillance for more than a year. After which time, no evidence was found for or against said crimes.

Finally, after a strong push for justice by the League of Pastors of New Orleans of all denominations, authorities decided that more drastic measures were needed.

It took nearly a year for authorities to infiltrate the cult with one of their informants, whose name will not be made known at this time, for safety's sake.

I have read the police report by the informant about what happened at these gatherings. Holding our readers in the highest regard, I cannot in good conscious convey the atrocities performed at these assemblies. I can only describe them as horrendous and unnatural.

Through the informant, it was known that this past Friday, they were to assemble at the home of Simon Peche. It was to be a high ceremony, on a particular satanic holyday.

A warrant was issued, and preparations were made for a raid on the cult. Police circled the home, so there would not be any escapes by any members.

However, it would seem the authorities were not the only ones with an informant. Peche and other members were all people of wealth and influence. Unbeknown to the authorities, the cult received word of the oncoming raid, at the last minute.

When the police knocked on the front door, there was no answer. It was then decided to use force, as the warrant allowed, breaking their way through the front door.

Immediately, it was apparent that none of the servants were in the house. With further inspection, the police came upon a large ballroom where the gathering had taken place.

All members of the cult were found dead, in a manner indicating a mass suicide. Later investigation proved this to be so.

It seemed they had engaged in a human sacrifice. The name of said victim is being withheld, as well as their gender and delicate age.

Again, to remain in good taste, I will not dictate the conditions of the dead members, only that it was evident they were victims of their own hands.

Captain Morgan of the New Orleans Police Department was quoted as saying: "This is surely the most horrific and unspeakable crime scene I have ever witnessed in my thirty years on the force."

A further investigation is ongoing, though little more is believed to be discovered.

1500 Lake Shore-Lake Vista has been sealed. An effort to locate any living relative of Simon Peche is underway. If no heir is found within the span of a year's time, the property will become city assets.

The names of the cult members found dead at the crime scene, including that of Simon Peche are as follows…

****

Winnie read off the names, silently in her head. Though it was a sad affair, she felt relief knowing that many of those involved in her past, the dark part of her life, were dead and gone. They would never be able to point a finger at her.

Although, a lightning bolt of fear rushed through her, as she read the names of the deceased. There was one very important name missing, that of Madame Charbonneau.

Forty-Four

Living in the Spirit

Life was beautiful in the Gibbs house, for staff and family. Jonathan worked every day for long hours. When he was home, Winnie was a part of almost every moment. Their love deepened in time.

Nearly friendless, Jonathan's world began to change. There were dinner parties held at the Gibbs home. In return, the couple was invited to the homes of others. Winnie and Jonathan became well-known socialites. It was suspected that Jonathan's newfound outgoingness was due to the joy he felt when showing off his beautiful wife. For whatever reason, good friends abounded.

Winnie was invited to many of the women's gatherings in high society about the city. She became a member of several lady's clubs and organizations. Not ever forgetting where she came from, Winnie spent a good amount of her time doing charity work.

All in all, the Gibbs were well-liked, respected, and admired.

****

Some might call it coincidence, some woman's intuition, Ma Cheri called it living in the spirit. No matter how you see it, there are occurrences in this life that have no explanation.

It was a common event, more than once per week; Winnie would head down to City Hall, where Jonathan worked, and lunch with him.

It was on this one particular day; Winnie declined a carriage ride downtown. It was such a love day, Winnie decided to walk. So, she left home early. She'd never walked the distance before, and had underestimated her walking ability. She arrived at City Hall, hours before lunch.

Having all this time on her hands, and not knowing what to do with herself, she thought she'd enter one of the courtrooms where court was in session. She'd often listened to Jonathan describe his day's work, only she never sat through a trial before. It fascinated her.

Taking a seat in the back, as not to disturb the goings-on, it was a good view of the entire courtroom.

The Presiding Judge was the Honorable Renault Lamar. An old man with long white hair, steel gray eyes, a stooped back, and a crimson, bulbous drinker's nose. Winnie knew little of the man, though he was one of the guests at her wedding.

Before the bench sat a frail-looking young black woman with her back to Winnie. The woman had no defense, nor was she allowed to speak on her own behalf. Winnie knew this to be strangely unfair and illegal.

One by one, witnesses were called on, swearing on the Bible, and taking the stand. Each in turn, spoke against the accused, pointing their finger at her, blaming her for so many crimes it was difficult to follow. They accused her of everything from petty theft, up to premeditated murder, and everything in between. Again, no one spoke up on the young woman's behalf, nor was she given a voice.

After each witness stepped down, Judge Lamar ducked down under the judicial bench. He was a sloppy drinker. They all heard him guzzling. As the trial wore on, Judge Lamar became drunker.

"Court will recess for lunch. We will resume in an hour," Judge Lamar announced at fifteen minutes to noon.

There were more witnesses to be heard. They were taking no chances. For whatever reason, it was clear they wanted the death sentence.

It was then, as they guided the prisoner back to her cell that Winnie got a good look at the woman's face.

My God, it's Jolene!

****

"My dear, what is the matter?" Jonathan asked, reaching across the table to her. "You haven't eaten a thing. You look like someone standing on the edge of an abyss."

Winnie looked out the window of Antoine's Restaurant, as she moved the food around in her plate with her fork.

"I saw something today that has wounded my heart. I can't stop thinking about it. And only you can help me," she answered softly.

"Of course, darling, name it and it's yours."

"I was in Judge Lamar's court this morning. There was a young black woman on trial. I know her. I know she would never do the things they're accusing her of doing."

"What is she accused of?"

"A number of things…the worst being murder…."

Jonathan released his hold of her hand, sitting back in his chair; he took in a deep breath, and then slowly exhaled.

"Winnie, I realize this is a friend of yours. And yes, I do have the power to reverse a judge's decision. Only, murder, Winnie, you don't know what you're asking."

"Jonathan, you know I love you, and I will continue to love you, no matter what you decide. Her name is Jolene Fairchild. I know in my heart she would never hurt anyone. I swear it."

"Winnie…I don't know."

"Jonathan, you've been more than good to me, but tell me when have I ever asked for anything? I'm asking you now to at least look into the matter."

Again, he sighed. "Very well, I'll look into the case, only I can't promise you anything."

"That's all I'm asking for."

****

The afternoon session in Judge Lamar's courtroom was a repeat of the morning session. Witness after witness swore on a bible, told the story of some heinous crime, and then pointed Jolene out as the perpetrator.

Again, Winnie sat in the back of the courtroom. She would have tried to get Jolene's attention, only the poor girl sat motionless, facing the court, and her head bowed down.

To hear how they slandered her was distressing. Not since the death of Belle had Winnie felt so helpless.

Without being given the chance to defend herself, two guards held Jolene before Judge Lamar. He disappeared under the bench for one last drink before passing sentence.

"Jolene Fairchild, you have been found by this court to be guilty of crimes against the laws of the state of Louisiana and society. You are a thief and a cold-blooded murderer. You are sentenced to be hanged till you are dead within twenty-four hours. May God have mercy on your soul."

The two guards dragged Jolene out of the courtroom. Judge Lamar staggered to his chambers.

Winnie rushed from the courtroom and up the stairs of City Hall to Jonathan's office.

"Winnie, darling, what's wrong? Why are you here?"

Winnie stood before him, shaking, crying. He rushed to her, taking her in his arms.

"Winnie, darling…?"

"Jolene hangs in the morning."

Forty-Five

Sisters

Jolene stood on the trapdoor of the gallows, the sack over her head and the noose around her neck. She breathed quickly, her heart pounding loudly, as if it might burst from her chest.

She heard the sound of someone rushing up the wooden stairs of the gallows.

"Here, read this," a voice said.

The next moment the sack was removed from her head, the scent of fresh air was as sweet as honey. They moved her off the trapdoor, as they removed the noose.

The guards guided her down the stairs and then back to her cell. There was talking all around her, nonetheless, none of it was directed to her. She was given no reason for the sudden reprieve.

In her cell, she knelt down, her hands folded upon her bed, praying prayers of thanksgiving and praise.

Hours later, the cell door opened. Two guards escorted her out and down the hall, and then through a door that lead out onto the street. Why they didn't cuff and shackle her, which they usually did whenever she was in transit, was one of many mysteries that she was too confused and frightened to ask.

Outside, they gently placed her in the back of a carriage, and drove off. In the most affluent part of town, they stopped before a three-story mansion. Taking her from the carriage, they brought her to the front door, and knocked.

****

Winnie was up early that morning, as excited as a small child at Christmas. She and Jonathan worked everything out in advance. She didn't eat that morning, full of anticipation.

When she heard the knock at the front door, downstairs, she rushed to the edge of the stairs to listen in. She heard Thomas, the head butler answer the door.

"Ah, yes, we've been expecting you. I can take her from here," Thomas told the guards.

When the door closed, Winnie heard them walking across the marble floor.

"What is this all about?" Jolene asked.

"It's not for me to say. All will become clear in a moment. Please, follow me," Thomas replied, guiding Jolene into the library.

Winnie tiptoed down the stairs. She stood at the doorway, listening.

The next moment, Thomas came out of the library. He smiled at Winnie as he passed her.

"Please, sit down," Winnie heard Jonathan say. "I'm sure you have many questions. My name is Jonathan Gibbs. I'm the City Judge. One of the duties of a City Judge is to oversee the rulings of the Municipal Court. I have the jurisdiction to override any of their rulings, which I've done in your favor.

"Why would you do that?" Jolene asked.

"Because I believe you are innocent."

"Why would you think that?"

"Actually, it wasn't me, it was my wife. She watched your trial. She believes you are not guilty. She's a good judge of such things. I trust her. But I want to hear it in your own words."

For the next hour, Winnie sat on the last step of the staircase, near the library door, listening to Jolene tell her tale of woe.

She opened fully to Jonathan, telling of every major moment in her life starting from when she was taken from her home up to the moment the noose was placed around her neck. She spoke about her time with Madam Charbonneau, where she was taught to be a *Fancy*. She told how she escaped from such a pitiful life, only to be the victim of an unwarranted hard life. Being accused for sins and crimes she never committed by the very people who performed the sins and crimes that they now point the finger at her for.

Winnie listened intently. Her eyes filled with tears, as she listened to the mistreatment that her adopted sister endured. Such a tragic life, no one should have to go through.

When she finished her account, all was silent.

Finally, Jolene spoke up. "I'm innocent of all wrongdoing, sir; I swear."

"No need to swear," Jonathan said. "I believe you. Now that I've heard it from your own lips, it only confirms what my wife told me all along."

Using her handkerchief, Winnie dried her eyes. Composing herself, she took in a deep breath, put a smile on her face, and entered the library.

"Ah, here is my wife, now," Jonathan announced.

So many years had passed; so much water under the bridge. Jolene did not recognize Winnie. All she saw was a beautiful woman, dressed in a gown fit for a princess. Sparkling diamonds adorned her neck and fingers.

"Did I not tell you, my darling, she was innocent?" Winnie proclaimed, taking a seat next to her husband, facing Jolene.

"Yes, you did, my dear," Jonathan concurred.

Winnie reached out, taking Jolene's hand.

"Has it been that long?" Don't you recognize your sister?"

Jolene leaned forward, searching her face.

"Winnie!" Jolene cried.

"Yes, but no longer just Winnie. I'm now Mrs. Gibbs," Winnie smiled at Jonathan. "I've worried everyday since the night I helped you over the wall of Madam Charbonneau's school. You were the sister I never had. I'm sorry for all you've gone through. If only I'd been there. All that will change from now on." Winnie turned to Jonathan "She can stay with us?"

"Of course, if it makes you happy," Jonathan replied with a smile.

"Yes, it would!" Winnie said, rising to her feet. Still holding Jolene's hand, she pulled her up.

"Oh, my dear sister…" Winnie shouted. The two women hugged, holding each other, in tears.

****

Many call it a coincidence, Ma Cherie would laugh at such a notion, calling it a miracle. Life in the Gibbs home became good, knowing happiness with no bounds. Both Winnie and Jolene traveled a long road of sorrow to get to a place of contentment.

True sisters they were, together, with Jonathan, they were now a family.

"If ever I'm a hindrance…" Jolene remarked to Winnie, as the two women looked out of the library window at the rainstorm whirling outside.

"Nonsense," Winnie declared. "Jonathan has grown to love you nearly as much as I do. You are my sister, from now until forever."

"But, if…?" Jolene concluded.

"No ifs, ands, or buts, my dear," Winnie said, the two holding hands admiring the storm outside. "You are my sister; and right now, I'm going to need you more than ever."

"How is that? Jolene asked.

Winnie turned away from the storm, smiling at Jolene. "I haven't said anything to Jonathan, yet. So, don't say a word, but, you are going to be an aunt."

THE END

Michael Edwin Q. is available for book interviews and personal appearances. For more information contact:

Michael Edwin Q.
C/O Advantage Books
P.O. Box 160847
Altamonte Springs, FL 32716
michaeledwinq.com

Other Titles in this series by Michael Edwin Q:

Born A Colored Girl: 978-1-59755-478-4
Pappy Moses' Peanut Plantation: 978-1-59755-482-8
But Have Not Love: 978-1-59755-494-7
Tame the Savage Heart: 978-1-59755-5098
A Slaves Song: 978-1-59755-527-5
Fancy: 978-1-59755-540-1
Wistful:978-1-59755-563-0

To purchase additional copies of these books visit our bookstore website at:
www.advbookstore.com

Longwood, Florida, USA
"we bring dreams to life"™
www.advbookstore.com